HENRY CLINE

SUMMONING THE GOWL-DIE

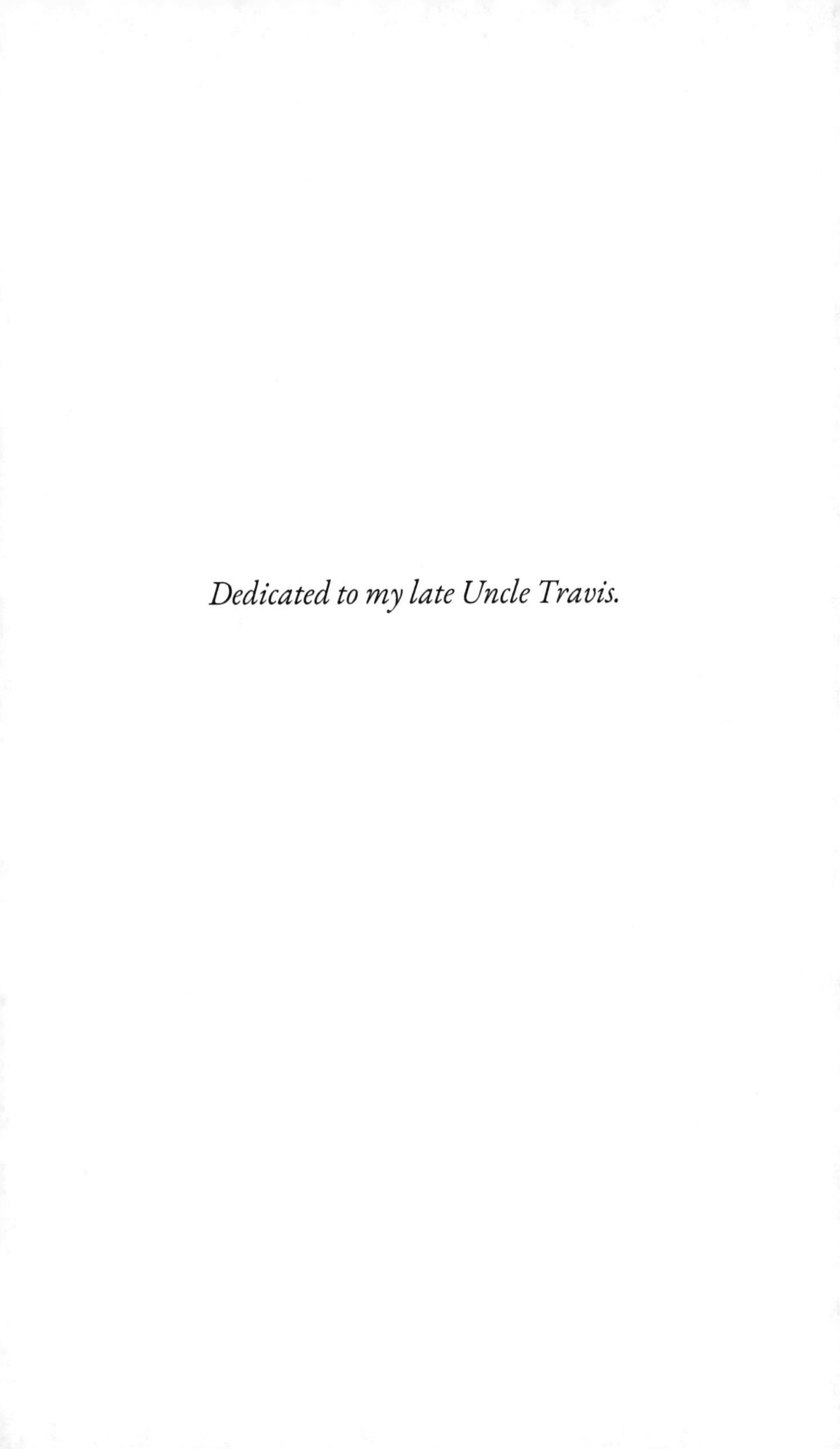

Dedicated to my late Uncle Travis.

TABLE OF CONTENTS

CHAPTER ONE

The Troublemaker

Elementary school, to middle, to high. I'd say during those first two parts of my childhood, I wasn't a troublemaker. In fact, I was the bullied one.

"You're so short!"

"You're so fat!"

"We have ourselves a pizza face over here!"

"Nice pants, gaywad."

It didn't help that I wore corduroy pants to school every day until I was 14 because jeans gave me a rash on my knees. So, that constituted the occasional beatdown on the playground. Or in a parking lot. Or wherever else. Y'know what they say, it was the "'80s." No one was safe.

Especially not in southwest Oklahoma, where I was born and raised. It was a smaller community, but everyone was either friendlier than you'd ever want them to be or they were hopped up on drugs or alcohol and ready to fuck your day up. Those kooky parents had kooky offspring, who tormented me at school or beat me up for being "short," "fat," and, I guess, "gay."

Anyway, what was I saying about corduroys? Oh, that's right. So, for some reason, something finally clicked when I turned 14, and I told myself, *no more corduroys*. And because of that, the gods granted me with puberty. Well, the rest of puberty. First, when I was 11, I was hit with acne, terrible body odor, and a lot of hair. But once I released myself from the shackles of those damned corduroys halfway through eighth grade, I was finally gifted with the growth spurt. And way less acne. And some muscles.

Payback time, right? Time to beat up all those who'd had it out for me growing up, right?

Well, wrong. But I had my reasons.

My dad always worked in the oilfields. Twelve-hour days, fourteen-hour days. I respected and feared him, even though I barely saw him most days. As for my mom, she changed jobs a lot as I grew up, but when I was in high school, she started making little trinkets and knick-knacks to sell on consignment at the corner store downtown. It didn't pay much, but she loved to do it. So much so, that even when I came home from the middle school beat-downs covered in dirt and bruises, she didn't pay me any mind. It was always the next stitch that mattered more. The next brush of paint. The next overly genuine depiction of an elephant's asshole for an egg-sized ornament.

Was fearing and respecting my dad why I didn't take revenge? I mean, it doesn't hurt to include that as a reason. But it was mainly because those bullies made friends with the new kid in town: Todd Pickley. And what did Todd Pickley's father do? As a matter of fact, Mr. Pickley was the field supervisor, a position that my dad had been working his way toward before it was yanked from him, which resulted in me playing an Atari while the other kids in school got Nintendo Entertainment Systems. At least, that was the only downside I saw.

As for my dad, he was stuck with the long hours, outside, almost losing a phalange, while Mr. Pickley sat in a nice trailer with state-of-the-art heat and air blasting away into his fat face all day, every day.

Okay, besides not getting an NES, I guess the other downside was that now I couldn't use my big muscles and testosterone to exact revenge. Instead, I had to deal with Todd and his gang of mutts 180 days out of each year. They gave me weekends off unless I ran into them in town. Oh, and holidays. So I guess they were pretty generous. But having to coop myself up every summer to avoid them was a bit maddening, to say the least. I became a momma's boy, having to assist with transporting her newest creations downtown, collecting the meager amount of money that she made on a given week, or sometimes having to help her paint the ornaments. I got to borrow the car at least, but there was a suppressed urge to drive into a large tree at 80mph to take myself out. Doing that would have ruined her creations, though (I'm not including myself in that statement).

Alright, enough of the whining. I feel that I've adequately summarized my childhood and teenage boy struggles. Poor me. But you might be wondering, *How are you a troublemaker if you haven't made any trouble?*

Well, I think it's time to move to the main event.

CHAPTER TWO

The Troublemaker's Mistake

April 1989
One month left of High School...

After an hour of listening to facts about the Korean War, it was time for lunch. I thanked God, as I was almost at my breaking point. I tried to be a good student. I made the best grades I could, and when the teacher was desperate to lock eyes with someone during a speech to make sure at least one person cared, mine were always available. Mr. Henderson needed them during the Korean War crap, I tell you what.

But lunchtime was bittersweet. Sure, I got to eat. But I also had to find either a tree or bench outside to eat at alone. Or I could sit with the nerds, they were always welcoming. Sometimes, I even sat with the Asians. But neither group would talk to me; it was just an empty spot. If I tried sitting with the jocks, or the cheerleaders, or anyone remotely popular, I'd be forcibly evicted. Not that I'd ever tried, but I saw it happen to others.

But thinking about my lack of popularity was too depressing.

Let's look on the bright side. Sloppy joes on a Thursday. I'll take it. One month left of school. I'll take it. And then, I'll...

Oh, that's right. I had only lied to my parents about wanting to go to college. And about applying to colleges. My older cousin, Alec, is considered the prodigy of the family. And that just from going to veterinary school. I did okay on my ACTs Sophomore and Junior years, but I never applied myself to take one again Senior year. The higher the score, the more colleges' eyes are on you. If my dad knew of my laziness, he would have signed me up for the armed forces by this point. Shooting

guns and blowing stuff up did sound cool, but signing up to kill others…
I don't know, my dad was lucky enough to have made it out of Vietnam.
I didn't know if I wanted to fight over a gulf, or a sea, or whatever.

Right when I decided to shove that thought process aside, I myself was shoved aside, by none other than Todd Pickley.

"Oops, sorry about that, Crisco."

Now, I'm not one to study bullying tactics, but it didn't really make sense that he still used an insult from my middle school days before he even attended school here—but I digress. It made his friends laugh, and that's all that mattered to him.

So, I had two options.

Option one: Stand up, grab the nearest lunch tray, and bash his face in. Downside, my dad would become unemployed and quite displeased.

Option two: Stay on the ground and let him say his piece. Downside, I look like a pansy. Yet again, I had to take the pansy route.

"Man, did I knock you down that hard? Do your legs not even work anymore?"

"Just leave me be, Todd."

"Ah, I see. Just lay down and take it. Kinda like your old man. I heard he wanted my dad's job before we moved to town, but uh, guess my dad had more qualifications."

Ooo, that hurt me more than I wanted to admit. But again, I couldn't say anything. I couldn't do anything. What could I actually do without landing in jail? That's the mindset I had to keep. Because I was tired of exchanging words. I wanted to act.

Luckily, my silence ended up boring him enough that he and his friends walked away. As cold as the tile floor was, I was starting to get comfy. Maybe I didn't need to get up and have lunch.

"Chris, are you okay?"

I didn't have the most unique name, so I figured whoever spoke was talking to someone else. However, I realized that someone was indeed talking to me.

It was Jasmine Farrah. She stood above me like an angel. Her long hair was tied back in a strict ponytail whenever she wore her pom squad uniform, made of mostly black, white, and red fabrics. MHS, Madison High School. Home of the Hornets. Wasn't going to be my home for much longer.

"Yeah, Jasmine, I'm okay. Thank you."

She reached her hand out to me. While looking at her hand, I noticed how smooth her legs looked. I was never this close to her on any given day. In fact, as she lifted me up, I tried to remember the last time I had even spoken with her or any other girl.

"Not a problem at all. Especially after you helped me with that English assignment."

Ah, that's what it was. Being the unsuspecting smart kid made a lot of people your friend. Mainly around testing time.

"Oh, the creative writing one? Yeah, I told you, that wasn't a big deal."

I started to walk away, but she stepped in front of me.

"No, you don't understand. Not only did Mrs. Harper love it, but I was able to send it in to Texas A&M!"

"What would they want with it?"

"Chris, don't be so dense! It was for a scholarship, and I got it!"

"Oh! Oh, wow. That's, uh, neat-o bandito."

"Not the terminology I was going for, but sure!"

Brushing my legs off, I decided the conversation was over and said, "Well, glad I could help."

Again, I tried to walk away, but again, she stopped me. This time, she put a hand up on my chest, and her voice dropped.

"Chris, I don't think you understand how much that helped me."

"No, you told me. It got you a scholarship. That's really neat."

Frustrated, she stomped her feet and said, "Well, we should go celebrate!"

Being from the Bible Belt, I almost thought she'd said "celibate."

But my brain kicked on, and I asked, "Celebrate? With ice cream or something?"

"No, I think we could celebrate a different way, right now."

Before I could say much else, Jasmine grabbed my hand, and we started heading toward the gym. Off-campus lunch wasn't allowed, so we weren't going out for ice cream. Or a snow cone. I really just wanted my sloppy joe, but I guess it would have to wait.

Her smile was infectious, but I had the vaccine. Food was all that was on my mind. What could be so important? Did she need me to do another assignment? No, she said we needed to celebrate.

It didn't click until we entered the empty gym just to find a mostly empty storage closet. In my defense, no girl had ever paid me any mind prior to this moment. And it finally hit me once she closed the closet door, turned on the overhead light, and stepped really close to me.

"I think you'll like this more than a sloppy joe."

As much as I wanted to interject that I was quite hungry, her soft, supple lips pressed against mine. I hadn't practiced sucking M&Ms off a mirror, so I had no idea if she was enjoying what I reciprocated. But the kissing continued, and she put her arms around me as her breathing heavied. I went ahead and put my arms around her as well, just as a courtesy. But of course, I had done something wrong.

"Chris, touch me."

"I believe I am."

"No, I mean..."

Taking her arms off of me made me feel like it was all over. However, when she stepped back and sat down on an old tanned leather folding chair, I knew there was more to come. She kept eye contact with me while slipping her shorts off from underneath her skirt. Her smile started to stray from innocent to lustful, while my mind went from hungry to horny.

"Give me your hand," she softly requested.

I could barely walk straight as I approached her. Something

underneath my belt was trying to make an appearance, but I didn't know if things would go that far. Trying to just live in the moment, I put out my left hand without asking questions. I knew basic biology, but not foreplay.

Next thing I knew, she pulled my hand under her skirt and up to her lower lady parts. I prayed she wouldn't know it was my first time doing all of this, but she probably did. She was giving me more direction than an air traffic controller.

Thinking back to any dirty movies I may have caught a scene from, I moved my left hand up, up, and away and started softly rubbing. People have made all kinds of comparisons to what a woman's parts are supposed to feel like, but it felt completely different from anyone's explanation prior. Unless Jasmine had a strange one.

She started softly moaning and kissing all over my face and neck. Monkey see, monkey do. I started kissing her neck but added in her ear. She was in shambles. Then, she said the number one thing that leads to teenage pregnancy.

"I want you inside of me."

Part of me wanted to say, "I believe I am," as I had before, but jokes weren't on the menu right now. She was looking down at my waist. Our hearts were pounding. We were completely alone, stuck in this moment together. No end in sight.

"Hey!"

It wasn't Jasmine's voice, and it definitely wasn't mine. I was glad I hadn't taken my pants off, but I couldn't say the same for her. Jumping away from her, I turned to the door and saw the janitor standing there. His eyes were about to pop out of his head, and I worried about where he was going to stick that mop.

"You two, get out of here! We're heading to the principal's office."

CHAPTER THREE

Consequences and Opportunity

"**I** don't even want to know what you two were doing in there, but I have an idea."

The principal started pacing behind his desk as he was talking to us. Jasmine and I were both seated while the janitor loomed behind us. They had already discussed what "may" have been going on. I just knew I was dead meat. There was no way to save myself.

"A month before school is over. One month before the two of you graduate. You try and have relations on campus."

I figured there was nothing I could say to save myself, so I replied, "Yeah, I'm sure no one has ever done what we did."

The comment stemmed from rumors about the school nurse getting handsy with the football team. Or other staff members acting in infidelity. One of those rumors happened to revolve around the very person who was about to determine our futures.

Principal Avrash looked like someone had stepped on his tail as he pointed his fat, stinky index finger at me.

"I have no tolerance for sarcasm."

"It wasn't sarcastic."

"Watch your damn mouth, Chris."

Unlike most people, if Avrash called you by your last name, you were friends. If he called you by your first, well, you're basically his mortal enemy. So, now that I knew where I stood, I really figured nothing mattered. Jasmine decided to add the icing to the cake.

"Principal Avrash, I swear to you, I didn't even know where Chris was taking me."

"Huh?" I blurted.

She was trying to save face. Maybe because it was covered in sweat and her makeup was smearing.

"Chris told me he needed help with a science project."

"And he led you to the gym closet?"

"Yeah, he said it was something about–"

"Bullshit!" the janitor said. "Whatever they were doing, she was into it, and he was in her, if you get what I'm saying."

"Jesus, did you impregnate this young girl?"

"I don't think my fingers can jizz."

At first, Principal Avrash didn't seem to know what jizz was. But he had enough context clues to put it all together, and I knew when he did as he let out a long groan.

"No, I'm serious. This was against my will. Principal Avrash, you ate with my father just a few days ago. Didn't he tell you I was going steady with Todd Pickley?"

Not even wanting to think about the repercussions of what she had just said, I replied, "Going steady? What is this, 1950?"

"I said, no sarcasm! If you really tried taking this girl against her will, I'm calling the police and expelling you."

And it was in that moment that I was done. That was it. I didn't know what scheme Jasmine was up to or why the principal would buy into it so easily, but I was completely done. In that moment, there was a sense of rebirth. I ignored the guilt of possibly getting my father in trouble, and I spoke my piece.

"Fucking do it, then!"

I was so proud of myself for not even stuttering or showing a shred of fear. Because I wasn't afraid. Well, going to jail as a rapist did scare me some, but I didn't plan on going easily. I knew I didn't do anything wrong. I knew this town was out to get me, for whatever reason. The bullying never stops, it just evolves.

"What did you say to me?" Principal Avrash exclaimed.

"Look, I don't care anymore, Have-a-rash. Expel me, call my dad, fuck my mom, I really couldn't care any less than I do right now. I'm expelling myself. Good riddance to you all.”

Avrash wasn’t the kind of guy anyone should mess with, but my rage seemed to throw him for a loop. He watched in a baffled state as I stood up, turned to the door, and walked out. The janitor seemed to give me a high-five with his eyes as I stormed out. What started as a slow march turned into a jog, even though no one followed me to my bike. I was fuming but satisfied. Any idea on what I would do next?

Nope. Just get to my bike.

That was my whole plan for the moment. My heart was beating tremendously, even more so than being with a pom girl, but not as much as if I had scored an actual cheerleader instead.

Sadly, especially in a small town like this, news travels fast. And as I squinted in the April sun while trying to get my bike unlocked, a low-IQ army marched up to me—it was Todd Pickley and his goon squad. I guess it wouldn’t be a proper goodbye without seeing him one last time. And, of course, he looked pissed.

“What is this I’m hearing about you and my girl?”

My padlock dropped into my hand, and I stood up to face him. No more Mr. Mute Guy.

“Your girl? You and Jasmine really do get along with your ’50s sayings.”

“Hah, you’ve been saving that one for the last four years so you wouldn’t get your daddy in trouble?”

“Eh, no, I found out about the sayings shortly after I finger-banged your ‘girl.’”

Todd’s entourage didn’t do him any favors as they hissed and laughed at my statement. Guess these losers could have been my friends all along. Damn, guess I missed out.

“You’re on thin ice,” Todd spat.

“What? As soon as I say something back, you hesitate? Have you always known that I had plenty of comebacks and can beat your ass easily?”

"Jasmine's pussy got him braindead," someone in the group said.

"Shut up, or I'll beat your ass next," Todd turned.

"Todd, one item at a time, man. You haven't even threatened me yet. I'm starting to feel left out," I replied calmly.

"Are you insane?" Todd asked. "Yeah, I'm gonna beat your face into a pulp. And then your dad is going to go home unemployed."

"Look, my face can take a beating. It has before. You, on the other hand... it'd be pretty devastating if you weren't as pretty anymore."

I was gripping my padlock this whole time. The loop was around my middle and ring finger. The extra weight would help, and before he could take his first sucker punch, I took mine.

As Todd opened his mouth, I threw a punch with all my might. I felt some teeth chip and cut into my fist as I yanked back. He didn't even react fully as I threw another punch, this time into his nose. His cartilage depressed under my fist a lot easier than I'd thought. And with a bloody face, he crumpled to the ground. Trying to avoid any of his loyal followers exacting revenge, I hopped on my bike and put the pedal to the metal. Only one guy seemed to gain speed on me, and I threw the padlock at his forehead. He went down instantly as well, and I started to wonder if I had gained superpowers.

I heard a few cars start up in the high school parking lot and figured the entire student body had been handed out a bounty for my head. If the payment was in sloppy joes, I'd turn myself in. But enough about wanting to eat. Some girl's twat had cost me my education and reputation. Now it was time to move. Make a plan. Get out of town.

My first smart move was biking through the wooded areas instead of taking the main streets. In fact, taking this route made even more sense as I had thought about going downtown. It would be more direct, even if it was bumpy. Then, once I was in town, maybe hop on the first bus out of here. If Avrash had called the police, they'd go to my house first.

So, goodbye to all my books, comics, and posters. I'll miss you, but I must leave you.

Wait, even if I make it downtown, I need money for a cab or a bus. All my lawn care money was at the house and, again, I couldn't go there. If only I had been a pirate and hid some money away in these woods.

Whipping through the trees, a thin branch made contact with my forehead and cracked off, which helped me think of the next step. I wasn't going to rob a store, but I could drop by the corner store and see if my mom had picked up her latest earnings. That's got to be enough for a bus out of town. Did stealing from my mom make me feel bad? Sure, but why not add to my growing list of degenerate activities? Eighteen years of being a good kid, I think I'm overdue on breaking bad.

The April showers from the night before didn't help with the stability of my route through the woods, but the trees helped keep any cars away from me. I didn't think they were any the wiser to where I was headed, anyway. Hell, I didn't even know where I was going until about five minutes ago. I was biking for my life, but I'm only human. My legs started to grow tired. My brain convinced them to keep working as I saw the back of the laundromat ahead of me. I felt close to my goal, although I wasn't sure what would happen after leaving town. Maybe my dad would hunt me down. Maybe Mr. Pickley would. No clue. All I could think was, get cash, haul ass.

Dropping from the high grass to the low concrete parking lot woke me up. I zipped through the mostly empty parking lot and approached the main street with caution. I jumped off my bike and started carrying it. Then, I pressed my back against the west wall of the laundromat and looked behind me. The woods were clear. Duh. I had just come from there. But in front of me, I didn't see any bounty hunters from the school.

They must all be heading to my house to burn it down.

Once I felt confident, I rode my bike across the street and zeroed in on the corner store. It was run by the Kelseys, and Chelsea Kelsey was the one I was hoping to see. Sure enough, as I walked my bike into the store, I saw the one, the only, Chelsea Kelsey. A cheesy name for a bright and bubbly gal.

"Well, Chris, good to see you!" she said from across the store. She finished folding a pair of jeans and then walked toward me. "Oh, honey, no bikes in here, please. Especially, by golly, did you just run that through the mud?"

"I was actually hoping to collect my mom's earnings and thought maybe you'd want to buy my bike as well."

Squinting with a bit of concern, she said, "I do have money for your mom. But honey, I don't buy bikes. Did you ask Al down at the pawn shop?"

Chelsea made her way behind the counter to fidget with a lockbox while I claimed, "Oh, yeah, Al, he, uh, said he has too many bikes."

"Too many bikes?"

"Yeah, he's spoke'en for," I joked, as my head spun around like a top, seeing if the police were onto me.

With a gasp, she replied, "What? Did he propose to that girl down at Jerry's Bar?"

If I have to explain the joke, it's not worth it.

"No, sorry, I misspoke."

"Hmm, is that because you like to ditch school and dirty up your bike?"

Chelsea handed me a wad of cash, mostly in fives.

"Oh, they let me off early today. Senior's day."

Chelsea made a face as she responded, "Senior's day? If you say so. Anyway, some funky fella came through here and bought a lot of your mom's merchandise. That's $80 right there."

In a bit of shock, I accepted the money. That was more than my mom made in the average month, and I had just picked up some money two weeks ago. Sure, it was wrong to take it, but I didn't have another choice.

"Wow, that's incredible. She'll be thrilled."

She sighed and brushed her blonde locks aside.

"Are you serious about selling that bike?"

"Yes, ma'am. $30."

"$30? But I have to clean it. How about $20?"

"Deal," I said, desperate to scrape up whatever cash I could.

"Okay, honey, let me go write up a receipt. Tell your mom congratulations and to make more stuff for me."

"Yeah, I hope that whack-a-doo comes in again soon. For my mom's sake, I mean."

Chelsea really didn't know what to make of me today, but she was willing to buy my bike. My anxious self waited for the measly $20. I was covering the "get cash" part of my plan. As for the second part...

The loudest rotary phone known to mankind erupted on the front counter of the store, breaking my train of thought. It didn't help that it was sitting on glass, adding to the jarring sound. Chelsea brought over a receipt book and said, "One sec, hun."

The internal bell still lingered as she lifted the phone, but it eventually died off.

"Hello?... This is Mrs. Kelsey... Oh, hi Robert... No, your sister isn't here, did you try the house?... Hmm, maybe she's at a doctor's appointment, I know her skin has been acting up... Uh huh... Well, I have her son here. Want to talk to him? Sure!"

A man named Robert, calling for my mom, but is okay with talking to me?

With no time to ask questions, Chelsea handed me the phone without any context or hints. I tried to think if anyone down at the police station was named Robert. Or if that was Mr. Pickley's first name. Before I could figure it out, I put my ear up to the phone to say, "Hello?"

"Chris, it's your Uncle Bob! Howdy!"

Oh, Uncle Bob. No one in my family called him Robert.

"Uncle Bob! Hi, hey, good to hear from you."

Damn, did the school call my uncle instead of my parents?

"Good to hear from you too, son. Say, I was hoping to talk with your mom, but maybe you could help me out instead."

My nerves were getting worse. The roar of a fiery siren made its way down the street right in front of the corner store, but it was just an ambulance. Probably for Todd.

"I'd be happy to try and help out."

"Great! Well, but you're probably still in school, aren't cha?"

"Uh," I started as Chelsea handed me $20. I mouthed a thank you to her and continued, "Y'know, it's funny you ask. I just got out of school today."

"Well, God is good, my boy. I was going to ask your mom, but I think you'd make more sense. I need a house sitter."

"Oh yeah?" I asked while a few cop cars sped by.

"Good Lord, what is going on out there?" Chelsea asked. "Are they heading toward the school?"

I exaggerated a shrug while Uncle Bob frantically explained, "Yes, sir. I got the most door-to-door sales in my department and my job appreciated my dedication and how many miles I put in, so they gave me and Misty an all-expenses-paid vacation!"

"A vacation? And all of it paid for? Wow, that's something special."

"You bet your ass! Now, they didn't give me much of a window, so I'm gonna have to beg ya to get out here ASAP. We need to ska-doodle on out of here pronto."

"Well, I am a working man."

"Oh, you'll get paid. I got $300 with your name on it right here at the house. One week. Misty is writing out some instructions for Mr. Pickles. Y'know, our cat."

"Of course, how could I forget?"

"Well, so, are you in? Or do I need to ask your mom to do it?"

"No, no, don't call her about it. In fact, I'll tell her before I leave, and then I'll be on my way."

"Son, you are a lifesaver. Honey! Chris can do it," Uncle Bob shouted. I heard my aunt cry out in joy in the background while Uncle Bob leaned back into the phone and muttered, "I mean, if it were up to me, I think the cat could survive without someone around for a week. But she insisted we find someone to watch the house."

"Uncle Bob, trust me. I'm your man for this."

"Now a firetruck?" Chelsea exclaimed as yet another siren filled the town. "I need to call my husband. Chris, can you wrap up the call?"

"Yeah. Hey, Uncle Bob, I need to drop off the line."

"Hold on, lemme give you the address. You're out near Lawton, right? We're up by Kingfisher off the Interstate a ways. You haven't been to our new house, have you? You're going to like it. But here's the address."

After giving me the address, we said our goodbyes, and I hung up the phone. Chelsea continued shaking her head as she said, "What is going on today?"

"No clue. But, uh, thanks for the money. See you around."

CHAPTER FOUR

The Troublemaker Gets Away

Living in a small town, there was only one cab driver around and he specialized in long trips. So, yet again, I was in luck. Even after fooling around with a girl at school, cussing out my principal, getting kicked out of school, and bashing my bully's face in, it seemed like someone was watching over me from above. Maybe it was due to my contributions to the thrift store and the associated church as a pre-teen. Of course, my mom actually got paid for her time, while I was just a "little helper," along for the ride.

I know all the stuff with my school had just happened, but it truly felt like time had skipped ahead a few years. Before today, I was already excited at the idea of school ending. But I never knew it'd happen like this, sitting in the back of a smelly taxi staring out at the open plains.

Mike, the cab driver, didn't ask too many questions. As long as I had the money, he didn't feel the need to know a damn thing. I liked that. And even though he didn't quite know the address I gave him, he knew how to get close enough to ask someone for directions.

Growing up, I had never really thought about getting out of Oklahoma. I still wasn't technically leaving, but I was leaving my hometown. However, I wasn't one to imagine leaving my hometown to travel to LA or NYC with dreams of becoming an actor or a musician. Either way, leaving Madison would suffice for now.

But what about after the house sitting?

Sure, I have an entire week to think about it. But is that really enough time to figure out the rest of my life? I suppose some people figure out their lives in a few seconds, especially in moments of uncertainty. If only I had figured everything else out while riding through the muddy woods.

"I don't go any faster than 60, and I don't feel like talking. Looks like you're traveling light," Mike commented.

"I'll use my imagination."

"Good."

That was about all we said to each other. And while he didn't feel like talking, he did have the occasional need to curse at other drivers. The only other time we conversed was about an hour into the trip. We were hit with some April showers, which resulted in both of us cursing as we wound the windows back up. I was fine with the rain. As long as it didn't mess the humidity up.

Oklahoma is quite known for its dry climate, whereas other places like Florida have wet climates. We weren't as dry as the desert, but I could definitely work up a sweat quickly on the wrong day. There's the USA State Comparison of the day.

With nothing else to do, my mind was wandering to all kinds of topics. I was just ready to be out of the cab, as I was becoming part of the reason it stunk to high Heaven. But we were able to take a break once we reached a dinky gas station in Kingfisher.

"I gotta ask for directions and take a piss. You wanna come in and get a snack?"

"That sounds good. As long as you don't leave me behind."

"Well, don't take too long picking out something to eat, then."

I was already out $60 from the ride. I didn't intend to spend $40 on snacks, but dipping into the remaining funds still unsettled me. But Mike had a lead on me, so I needed to head in.

The grimy glass door to the dilapidated structure swung open with zero resistance. The hinges must have been the only thing not covered in muck because everything else seemed to be. Well, besides the groceries on the shelves. They just had the occasional web.

"Got a key for the pisser?" Mike asked.

"You ain't shy, are ya?" the owner replied as he reached about for the key.

"Nope. But while I piss, how about you tell this young man how to get to his uncle's house?"

Mike shoved his map and the note with my uncle's address to the clerk in exchange for the bathroom key. Once Mike was out of the picture, the gas station owner said to me, "Hmm, okay. Oh, that's that Ruby Falls edition they made 'bout five years ago. Those are nice. Are you familiar with these parts?"

I shook my head as I looked for a candy bar.

"I'll just wait for your driver to return, then. No sense in telling you."

"Yeah, I'm just a dumb ole kid, after all."

"I can tell."

I didn't have the same distaste for the clerk as I did for Todd, so I didn't punch his face in. Besides, he's the only one that could tell us the directions to Uncle Bob's house. That's what I told myself, anyway.

I grabbed a few candy bars, some chips, some granola bars, and a soda. When I stepped up to the counter again, the owner took a long look at me and said, "I didn't mean anything about what I said earlier. Just had some fella earlier that kinda ticked me off. Had a weird presence about him, can't quite explain it. But I can tell you're a kid with what you're buying."

"Well, what do you suggest?"

"Oh, that depends. You're heading to a friend's house or, oh, you said your uncle's, right?"

"Yeah, it's my uncle's house. I'm watching it for them while they go out of town. An extremely last-minute thing."

"Is that so? Well, in that case, I'd grab some hot or cold cereal and milk. Hopefully, they have some canned goods for you, but milk spoils. And if it's that last minute, well, who knows what they have for you to eat? Also, I have some traveling toothbrush kits over there. Get one of those. Maybe a frozen pizza, too. I'll say a prayer for you. Hey, now that I mention that..."

Digging around in some old papers, he found a pristine pamphlet and handed it to me.

"... that fella I mentioned before. Well, now, I am a God-fearing man. But when he was done ticking me off, he invited me to some church I'd never heard of. Must be new. But if you're unfamiliar with this town, maybe you should attend. Especially if you're here for the next week. Sunday is right around the corner."

Uh, if he doesn't want to go, why would I?

But I had to admit, the pamphlet was intriguing. My whole life was filled with invitations to Catholic, Methodist, Baptist, Lutheran, and Pentecostal churches. But this pamphlet was different. It didn't have a nice sky-blue background, but instead, the front showed an old-looking building over a dry brown background. When I say old, I mean ancient. It didn't look exactly like a photo, but if the physical location was anything like the image, it had no stained glass, no steeple, nothing. It looked like an old 1920s schoolhouse that was being used as a church. Plus, the fact that it was depicted as a darkly colored church implied something sinister to me. Trying to understand clearer, I read the bottom of the flier.

"'The Church of New Beginnings,'" I muttered.

"I've already been baptized, that's why I declined the offer. I don't need a new beginning," the shop owner explained. "Plus, he didn't specify the denomination."

"Interesting," I replied.

No, truly, I was interested, and opening the flier didn't do me any favors.

Hello! Are you feeling lost or wanting to join a strong community? We hope you can join us this coming Sunday for our service. Pastor Blackwood and his family would be delighted to have you attend and hear stories of the next coming. Bring yourself, or bring your family, as we set out to entertain and captivate you with stories and proverbs of old and new. And, hopefully, you will stay as part of our army.

Army?

"Hey, did you tell the kid how to get to his uncle's?"

Mike let us know he was back from the bathroom. He placed the key on the counter in exchange for his map. The owner said, "No, I was going to wait for you. Kid doesn't know this area. Here, let me check him out and bag up his goodies, and I'll explain the way."

CHAPTER FIVE

Ruby Falls

At exactly 5pm, we finally arrived at my new temporary home. My uncle's neighborhood was about 20 minutes from that gas station, and the road to get there was mostly gravel. The rain over the previous few days didn't help with the traction on Mike's old taxi, and when he finally pulled onto actual asphalt before entering the neighborhood, he sighed with relief.

Ruby Falls was a mix of old and new. The entrance was on the southwest side, with pretty signage announcing the name. The paint on the sign appeared to be fresh, with bright red used for the text and an ocean gray for the rest. The houses appeared to have been built in a U-shape on one continuous street, with maybe 20 houses total. Five to the west, five in the middle of the U, five to the north, and five on the far right. Those living on the far east side had to come around the entire U anytime they needed to go somewhere. Knowing my Aunt Misty, that would have driven her nuts. If she wanted to go somewhere, it was now or never. Maybe that's the real reason they were in a rush to leave.

I couldn't see every single house to the east, as there was a heavy forest surrounding the entire neighborhood and random groupings of trees around each house. By the end of March, most of Oklahoma's vegetation is popping with green—this neighborhood had photosynthesis working overtime, with a blinding amount of chlorophyll being produced. Uncle Bob was right about two things: I hadn't seen their new house yet, and I felt I would like it.

After passing the entrance, Mike stopped the taxi and opened a new pack of cigarettes.

"Alright, kid, you're here."

"Oh, are they the first house on the left or right?"

"No, not the first. They're the last house on the left."

"Okay," I said, not really sure what his logic was. "So, why are you stopped at the entrance?"

"Because I'm tired and need to get back. You can walk, can't you?"

"Yeah, sure. Thanks."

After releasing my rage on the principal and Todd, I seemed to be able to give everyone else a pass. Part of me wanted to mouth off to the gas station owner for calling me a dumb kid, and part of me wanted to tell Mike off for dropping me so far away. Each house had about an acre between them, which wasn't going to kill me, but I wasn't thrilled. Whatever. Might be my last time seeing Mike, might as well leave it on a good note.

I began to step out with my bags of bullshit, but before I closed the door, I said, "Hey, Mike, I'd appreciate it if you could keep this trip between you and me."

The effort he made to twist his body around at the waist was over the top, but once he was settled, he said, "You're not the first person I've had to drive last second out of town. I just hope you didn't rob a bank or kill anyone."

I was sure about the first thing, but wasn't sure about the second. I nodded, patted the roof, and closed the door.

The weather was a perfect mix of overcast and breezy as I started my way down the street. For a name like "Ruby Falls," there wasn't a lot of red to be seen aside from the sign. And if there were gemstones underneath the ground, I'd start digging as soon as I got to their house. Instead, fighting against the evergreen grass and trees were white and yellow flowers in most flowerbeds. The homes themselves all looked relatively new, but they all appeared to have wooden fronts and brick on all other walls. The wooden fronts were either a muted cream color, a muted brown, or a muted mute color.

I could see my uncle's house at the end of the street, and sure enough, it was more of the same. Only difference was that my uncle's house wasn't two-story. Either everyone had two stories, or it was an optical illusion. I couldn't see any 19th-century expressionists making houses in Kingfisher, OK, but I guess you could never know. All in all, the houses were nice. Everyone must have coordinated to cut their lawns on the same day because they all appeared identical. Everything seemed cookie-cutter. Even when I unassumingly peered into a few homes, I saw couples or families sitting down for dinner. All well-dressed, all smiling and happy. There didn't seem to be any concerns within the households, and for some reason that bothered me.

My dad always came home angry, and my mom was always flustered with paying bills and balancing the checkbook. There were moments of peace, like if my dad got a few days off for bad weather or a dry site. Well, I take that back. If he was home, I wasn't allowed to play hooky without him keeping an eye on me at all times. He never believed I was sick, even if I was running a fever. His solution for sick people was to stay in bed like some near-death patient. And as soon as I would get up to do anything, the validity of my illness was questioned.

I didn't hate my dad by any means. Or my mom. They're just parents. And until you turn 18 and live out on your own or you don't have to ask them for any money, the relationship stays strict. I did feel a bit of guilt about maybe costing him his job, but he could definitely find other work. He was a hardworking, well-rounded man. Maybe he could start fixing up cars downtown with Greasy Jerry.

My right hand started to sting as I carried the groceries. I looked down and saw the bruising around my fingers where the padlock was. First, I grimaced at the pain, then I smiled at the thought of Todd being on the ground. Pros and cons.

It wasn't much longer before I stepped onto my uncle's lawn. I had never been informed of the new purchase, and my family was never sent any photos of the place. But the address matched the one I wrote down at the corner store. The only house with a low roof. I walked to the front door and saw Mr. Pickles' gray and white fur pressing against the front window. That solidified the ownership of the house, unless Mr. Pickles was a home invader. As I approached, he cocked his head and offered a soft meow. I gave him a nod and placed the groceries down at the dark red front door. Finally, something red in Ruby Falls.

My uncle was my mom's brother, but I remembered him talking to my dad about keeping a key outside his house. I checked under the doormat and there was nothing but dirt. Then, I checked under some flower pots. Still, no good.

That's when I saw that the "No Solicitors" sign was crooked. Turning it around revealed the plain brass house key. Tucking the sign under my arm, I unlocked the front door and lifted the groceries to head inside. And once I was in, I locked the deadbolt.

There wasn't a single lightbulb on in sight. With all the clouds outside, it made parts of the house barely visible. The front entryway was wide with tanned wallpaper, along with a hardwood table for the mail or keys. For now, it would hold the solicitor's sign as well as the house key.

Unlike most cats, Mr. Pickles came out to greet me from the room on my left.

"Hey, pal, long time no see."

As he brushed up against my leg, I reached down to scratch his cheek. He was an indoor cat. Aunt Misty had told me that if they did let him outside, someone would absolutely steal him based on his manners.

The room he was in was a formal dining room, with a twelve-seater cedar table. I wasn't sure who else in my family lived out this way, but Uncle Bob seemed to be prepared to host any future holiday. Not a bad thing, but it didn't match the way his old house was. In fact, as I walked into the dining room and out the adjacent side to the living room, none of their furniture or wares looked to be carried over from the previous house. Everything appeared to be brand new. Thinking back, they used to have a bookshelf with a few cigarette burns on it. Something about Grandpa Smitty pissing off Grandma. However, the bookshelf in their house didn't have any burns or stains or character. Rather, it was in pristine condition. Also, their couch had very few scratch marks where the previous one had plenty of Mr. Pickles' marks. Not to mention some of his fluids were on the old couch, too.

The entire place really struck me as odd. My critical thinking skills wanted to evaluate why they couldn't afford a vacation until something happened at work, when all the furniture, appliances, and overall decor could have paid for a few vacations at this point. But, it wasn't my place to say.

The house just didn't feel as comfy to me. I even worried that I was in the wrong house, and that Mr. Pickles *was* a home invader. Trying to be more logical, I figured they maybe just decided to go out with the old and in with the new. But I knew my mom and her sister would be mad if they weren't offered any of the old furniture that my grandfather had made, and sometimes, put out cigarettes on.

Misty sure kept the place clean, as well. My jeans already had remnants of cat hair stuck to them as I walked from the lavish living room to a more contemporary kitchen. Opening the bottom section of the fridge, there was a carton of eggs, some cheeses, lunch meat, and sweet tea. No milk.

"Good call, gas station guy."

Then I checked the freezer. Some hamburger patties, bacon, and ice trays. I threw the frozen pizza in and closed the door.

With the refrigerator door still open, I checked over the rest of my items in the shopping bag. Standard procedure was to take each item out of the grocery bag and place them in their respective spots. This time, I just threw the entire grocery bag into the fridge, closed the door, and put it out of my mind.

It was when I stood up straight that something fluttered in the corner of my eye. Turning to the sink, I didn't notice anything at the window overlooking the backyard, but I approached to make sure. Seemed like a shadow, but for what creature, I did not know. Was it human or animal?

Well, it turned out to be nothing. I mean, it was something, but nothing to fear. In addition to Mr. Pickles, they also owned about six chickens. Granted, I was high on adrenaline when I talked to my uncle, but I was pretty certain there was no mention of chickens.

The door to the backyard was in the living room, so I decided to step out and look around. Mr. Pickles wanted to come along, but he had murder on his mind as he glared at the chickens. As for me, I was just curious. Closing the door behind me, I took a few steps onto their concrete porch and stopped. Again, they had a few too many chairs for the two of them. Two separate metal tables were placed under the awning with four matching metal chairs each. If they weren't hosting other family members, maybe they were having the neighbors over. This was a pretty isolated community, so what else could they do except stay here or go into town?

There was one thing that didn't look brand new, and it was Uncle Bob's charcoal grill. I opened it just to have some charcoal dust fly up in my face. In a coughing fit, I dropped the handle, making plenty of noise. The chickens scattered before I could even go look at them. But they couldn't escape. The backyard had six-foot-tall wood fencing on the north and south sides, with steel bars for the posts. The west side of the fence was shorter and diamond-faced, which made sense. If they had gone with the gargantuan wood all the way around, it would have blocked out the hauntingly beautiful woods.

I coughed once more and started to pat myself down, but a feeling similar to when I saw the shadow out of the corner of my eye started to creep in on me. Someone or something was watching me. Was it out in the woods?

I was thinking the shadow from before was a chicken that could get some air, but that didn't really make sense. Chickens can't fly, so…

"Hehe."

My head whipped to the south. I missed it at first, but then I saw the top half of some kid's head, peeking over the fence.

"Oh," I said, somewhat relieved.

I couldn't tell what the little boy's facial expression was, even though it seemed like he had just laughed. I figured he found my charcoal incident hilarious. But the laugh from before was soft, but not soft enough for someone trying to make himself unknown.

As I waited for the kid to say something, the chickens appeared to scatter again. Nothing had audibly disturbed them, so I wondered why they ran off. But then, the kid just kept staring, and I started to piece something together.

"You didn't just come over here, did you? And look in the kitchen window?"

"Nope."

"Did you see anyone else?"

Not interested in my line of questioning, he replied, "You're new."

"Huh?" I replied, confused. He wasn't long-winded for a kid. After I took a second to think about it, I went, "Oh, yeah, you got me there. I'm watching my uncle's house."

The kid's green eyes didn't move. He continued staring at me, almost like he was scanning me. Eventually, he jumped down from the fence into his own yard and said, "New is good."

I stood there, trying to make sense of what he meant. In the end, I scoffed, patted myself off a bit more, and muttered, "He must really not like my aunt and uncle."

CHAPTER SIX

Recovery

After the backyard incident, I took a quick shower in the guest bathroom and dug around for clothes in their guest closet. Uncle Bob kept some of his high school shirts in there, and they were only a little baggy on me. I even scored some pajama bottoms. And once I got back to the living room, I hopped on the couch. Before I could reach the TV remote, Mr. Pickles cuddled up on me, and his soft snore reminded me how tired I was.

So, I ended up passing out, right there on the couch. And even though I forgot to close any of the blinds, I didn't wake up until about noon the next day. Having a chunky cat pressed on my mid-torso all night didn't make it the most restful sleep, but I guess I needed it if I slept about 15 hours. When I woke up, I couldn't remember if I had any dreams or not. I did know that propping my back up against the end of the couch with one tiny pillow in my lower back was bad for my neck. Blood flow to my head should have stopped at some point, but I was okay for now. After sitting up, I popped my neck from left to right and felt some relief. I heard the faint sound of Mr. Pickles munching on kibble, and I wondered if he needed a refill.

The clouds weren't as stagnant as yesterday. They were racing each other to see who could cover the sun up next. At some point, while I was in the shower, one of their living room lamps had come on with a timer, and turned off sometime while I was sleeping. But with it being midday, the house didn't need a bunch of lights on.

The kitchen had a smaller dining room table for four, and I guessed my aunt and uncle ate most of their meals in there rather than the formal dining area. They had dark purple woven placemats at each spot, with a nice floral centerpiece. The flowers were fake, so I wouldn't have to bother watering them. But there was a note near the centerpiece that I had missed the night before. I picked it up and started reading Aunt Misty's cursive.

Chris, thank you so much for watching the house while we're gone. A few things:

The chickens are self-sufficient. They should have plenty of feed.

Mr. Pickles has extra food out in the garage. He was getting bad about ripping into the bags if we left them out on the counter.

Sleep in our room or guest room. Doesn't matter, but our bed has more room for you and Mr. Pickles.

If Bob tells me a phone number for where we're staying, I'll write it and the hotel number here before we leave. _______________________________

Love,

Misty & Bob

"Guess she didn't have time to write down a hotel name or number," I commented as I placed the paper back down. My disappointment changed to glee as I spotted a few $50 bills poking out from the centerpiece. I smiled, crammed the cash in my pajama pocket, and sighed. I figured they would call me if anything serious came up. Surely, they knew their own phone number.

Mr. Pickles was up on the cabinets near the sink. I almost scolded him until I saw his food and water dishes were up there. As he chomped away, I figured I'd leave him be.

Down the hall toward the bedrooms was a guest bathroom, where I had taken a shower the night before. Now that I had permission to go into their bedroom, I was curious. Turning right at the end of the hall, I faced their slightly ajar bedroom door. I went ahead and pushed it all the way open to explore.

As a kid, I was really bad about digging around family members' houses. Especially if I was left alone. One time, there was a medical emergency at my grandparent's house, and all of us kids were left at home alone. Some of us found rated-R movies while the rest of us rummaged around. We made sure not to leave too much evidence before they got back, though.

Now, as an 18-year-old, I was well aware of rated-R movies, and even some X-rated. But that's not what I was interested in now. Passing their chest of drawers on the left, I walked in to see their massive bed.

"Must be one of those California Kings everyone is raging about," I slighted.

Besides that, they had a variety of family photos on the walls, ranging from black and white to color, from small to large, and rectangular to square. There were a few of me and my cousins, and a classic photo of my mom and dad when they were first dating, along with a photo of Bob and Misty in their 20s. My mom was turning 40 this year, so that meant Bob was about 43. If this was his birthday trip, I felt a little bad about the money he'd left me. Oh well. Now, I could pay my mom back once I was halfway across the country.

The bedframe was low to the ground, and the oversized comforter made the drawers underneath almost unnoticeable. But as I said, 18 or not, I was still a kid at heart and wanted to poke around. I'd come back later.

The bathroom in the hallway had a half-n-half tub and shower. The master bath, however, was a massive jacuzzi-style tub and a walk-in shower, with black-and-white tiles and cream-colored walls.

"I'm gonna have to scrub-a-dub-dub in here next time."

Otherwise, there wasn't much to see. Therefore, I left the bathroom to enter the bedroom once more. Four drawers to go through. I tried to guess which side was my Uncle Bob's. I figured he had the nightstand with a few magazines on it, while the other side of the bed had some actual novels. Hoping the cabinets wouldn't be home to anything too risqué, I walked up to the side closest to the entryway of the bedroom and pulled the top right drawer. At a glance, it was a bunch of extra bedding in various color schemes. Boring.

I went down and opened the bottom right drawer. Loose leaf paper was strung about, none of it filed or sorted in any particular way. Everything from Bob's military service to the last few years of tax returns. What a mess.

Finally, I moved over to the left-side drawers and opened the top one.

"Holy shit."

Mr. Pickles meowed at the doorway, seeming to agree with my surprise at what I was seeing. The short version is guns. The long version, my uncle had a silver 1911 pistol, a pump action short-barreled shotgun, a 357 revolver, a smaller revolver, and a field-ready lever action rifle that was broken down into two easy-to-fit pieces. Otherwise, the rifle in its assembled state would have been too long for the drawer.

"Pretty sure you only have two hands, Uncle Bob. Not sure why you need all this firepower."

Looking up temporarily, I felt blind and dumb as I saw Mr. Pickles rubbing up against a gun safe on the other side of the bedroom. I took a quick peek in the bottom left drawer to find nothing but ammo, then made my way to the gun safe.

I didn't know what I was going to find. Well, except for more guns. But maybe not. The gun safe was over on Aunt Misty's side of the bedroom. Maybe it was used for arts and crafts.

And while I thought the whole point of a gun safe was to keep it locked, the metal door swung open easily and revealed yet another arsenal. Bolt action rifles, semi-auto rifles, and his 10-gauge pump-action shotgun that almost blew my shoulder out as a kid. Several magazines filled to the brim, along with some other accessories that looked like grenades. I knew what all the guns were because I was a typical midwestern boy, but damn. Picking up an M16A2 out of curiosity, I released the magazine and cleared the round in the chamber. He had it locked and loaded, with the safety off and the switch turned to...

"Full auto?"

Is he allowed to have this because of his time in the military, or am I holding a felony?

I didn't have time to decide. A loud knock at the front door made me physically jump, and Mr. Pickles hissed while running under the bed. Looking at the bedroom clock, it was around 1:30pm. On a Friday. Who the heck would be knocking on doors?

Wait, why did Uncle Bob have all these guns? Did he have all these at his last house?

Confusion and concern started to take over me. I had an inkling that I should grab a gun, but I couldn't open the front door with an M16. I placed the rifle back into the gun safe. I wanted to just head straight to the door, but the inkling became a massive stain on my mind. I started thinking about why Uncle Bob would want all these guns, or need them. Sure, 2nd Amendment, yeah, yeah, yeah, but did he feel threatened here?

The guns were making me paranoid, and I made an executive decision to be armed when I answered the door. Going back to the bed frame, I opened the drawer and grabbed his 1911. When I put it in the pocket of my pajamas and took a single step, my pajama pants fell around my ankles at the weight of the gun.

"Shit," I mumbled as I placed the 1911 back in the drawer and grabbed the small revolver instead.

Someone was pounding away at the front door while I struggled to pull my pants up. But once they were up, I tied a lazy knot and held the revolver in my left hand. It wasn't my dominant hand, but at least I had it ready.

Finally, I took a breath and opened the door halfway to reveal...

"Hi, package for Misty... Oh, I was pretty sure I was at the right house?"

It was the damn postman with a package for my aunt. I slipped the revolver into my left pajama pocket and opened the door further.

"Yeah, hi, I'm their nephew. They're out of town."

"Oh, okay. Hi, nephew. Just need a signature. She already missed this package the first time so that's why I knocked extra loud."

"Trust me, I could hear you."

The postman handed me a booklet to sign off that I had received the package, and then handed the box to me.

"Oh, and their mail for today."

The postman reached into his satchel, tossed some mail on top of the box, and bid farewell. I stepped back, closed the door with a sigh of relief, and locked it.

I hated to blame the guns for making me paranoid, but it was definitely the guns. Scared of a damn postman. Well, in my defense, it was my first time house sitting for anyone. I had been home alone before, but not like this. Not at a house that practically felt like a stranger's.

Mr. Pickles came up to rub against me and purr my anxieties away. I placed the box down on the front entryway table and took the mail to thumb through it, just to simulate being a homeowner. Heading toward the kitchen to make a snack, I observed a utility bill, a few coupons for a grocery store out of town, and then, something I was already familiar with.

The pamphlet for The Church of New Beginnings. The exact same one from the gas station.

"What the..."

It wasn't even stamped or anything. Didn't the postal service only distribute pieces of mail with stamps? No "To" or "From." Just the pamphlet in its unaltered glory. I kept reviewing it, and as much as I hate to admit it, the pamphlet jarred me so much, I didn't even think twice about there now only being five chickens in the backyard instead of six.

CHAPTER SEVEN

Uncertainty

The rest of my Friday night was nothing too special. Finding a basketball game on TV helped fill the silence in the house, but I wasn't actually interested in the game itself. Both teams had two wins each, and it was the finals; Game six or seven would be the exhilarating one, not game five.

The oven stunk to high heaven as I cooked a frozen pizza on the middle rack. I wondered if Aunt Misty's cleaners had dissolved by now, if she did indeed clean the house prior to my arrival. I mean, it did smell nice when I walked in. If she didn't, the 400-degree oven would certainly kill any lingering bacteria, right?

Mr. Pickles was up on the counter, munching away at his dinner. While I waited for the timer to go off, I peeked my head around to check the TV. Maybe I did care more about watching the game than I cared to admit. But it was nice to have something to put my mind on, especially after the encounter with the mailman. Sure, he seemed nice enough, but I didn't understand why he would be helping distribute the flyers of this church without actually speaking on their behalf. If he was a member, why didn't he provide a spiel of some sort to convince me to join? Maybe their method was as simple as dropping it off and letting you think it over yourself, just like I was doing now.

Sounding unhappy, Mr. Pickles let out a cry, and I looked over. His food bowl was fine, but he didn't have any water.

"Sorry about that. I should probably hydrate myself, too."

When I first turned on the sink, the water that expelled from the faucet was a murky brown. I waited, knowing this issue from back home. Soon enough, the water changed to a more appealing color, and

I rinsed Mr. Pickles's water bowl of any excess hair or bits of food. While I rinsed the bowl, I looked through the window to see the chickens trot about. It was another pastime of mine at my uncle's house, but it didn't help with the quiet. At least they didn't have a rooster to wake me up every damn morning.

Letting out a cry again, Mr. Pickles reminded me that the bowl didn't have to be perfect. I finished filling it up and placed it back on the counter for him. After a pat on the butt, he went for the water. I couldn't even remember the last time I drank water. I was living on soda and tried one of my uncle's beers last night, but it was flat. Time to drink some actual water.

I downed a glass, and the kitchen timer went off. Pizza time for me. They had a circular sheet pan that should help me shovel the pizza out. It took a bit of finesse, but it eventually got onto the pan, and I placed the pan on the stove. I was willing to wait, oh, about ten seconds for it to cool while I poured myself another glass of water. But with my beverage ready, it was time to cut the pizza. Oddly enough, they didn't appear to have a pizza cutter. Looking around, I found their fancy cutlery and grabbed a nice chef's knife. It wasn't serrated, and I found as the pizza moved back and forth with my cutting motion, it took a considerable amount of time to make any progress. Once I was done cutting half of it up, I placed it on a plate and tried to ignore all the cuts I left on their pan.

With a plate of poorly sliced pizza in one hand and a glass of water in the other, I made my way to the couch. It was one of those couches that never wanted you to leave, so I made sure I had everything before sitting down.

Well, I forgot napkins, but I can just lick my fingers.

I put my glass of water on the end table and tried taking a bite of pizza. I found it was still way too hot as I regretted that first bite. Mr. Pickles watched as I writhed in agony, then decided to jump up on me to make me feel better. I mean, I thought he wanted me to feel better, but instead, he wanted a bite of pepperoni.

"Oh, that's how you do it, huh? You little charmer."

His pupils were wide, and the purring was intensifying. I made it a staring contest at first, but he won. Ripping off a piece of pepperoni, I bit off half and tossed him the rest. I didn't think about the sauce getting on the couch until it was too late. He seemed to clean it up pretty nicely, though. And once he was done, he came back for more.

"Hey, I think you already ate tonight, whereas I, on the other hand…"

Oh, he didn't care what I had to say. He was just thinking about taking my fingers off if I didn't offer pepperoni anymore.

"Fine, here."

I did the same thing: Took a piece of pepperoni, bit off half, tossed the other half. We made it a game for a while, but after he had eaten the equivalent of three pepperonis, he gave up and fell asleep on my lap. Floating the plate above his head, I continued eating my four slices of pizza and debated on getting the other four from the stove. The game was getting good, though, and they had just come back from the third quarter. I could hear my mom's voice telling me to wait and see if I was truly hungry or just bored.

She'd also be amazed that I was watching basketball. I was really more of a comic book dweeb, but my aunt and uncle didn't appear to have any comics for me to read. I was always locked up in my bedroom unless I was out in the living room or kitchen to prove I was doing my homework. Having a house all to myself was completely out of the ordinary.

Then, with the mention of the unordinary, a series of events happened faster than I could process. A grotesque shrill came from the backyard, a sound like I had never heard. I remembered one of my teachers in elementary school let us have a class chicken, but I had never heard one make that noise. Soon afterwards, the entire house experienced micro power flashes, and the TV's volume practically exploded. The mix of the unidentified shrill along with the blaring TV made me drop my pizza plate on Mr. Pickles, who had been in a deep sleep. When the plate bounced off of him, I reached down to reassure him it was an accident, but he brandished his claws and swiped. Since I reached down to him with the back of my hand, he slashed at it before making a run for it. Now, the TV turned completely off, and the image began to fade, but the other lights in the house stopped flashing.

What the hell was that?

Well, pizza stains were the least of my worries now. My right hand was gushing with blood all over the couch and rug underneath. This wasn't a mess I felt comfortable licking up, so I started cursing at myself and ran to the kitchen. I grabbed a washrag and wrapped it tightly around the wound, and that would have to do for now. It was already dark outside, so I couldn't see out the kitchen window, but I planned to go outside and look around.

This time, I grabbed the 1911 pistol with my left hand and turned the back porch lights on. Then, I placed my bloodied right hand on the door handle to the backyard but started to question my decision to go outside. Deciding to stay close to the house, I took a deep breath and opened the door.

Stepping outside didn't help my nerves. I closed the door behind me and switched the pistol to my right hand, even though the rag didn't help my grip. Once my feet touched the grass, I stopped moving. The air was thick and still, with a gross humidity that was dying out as it got later in the day. My brain and imagination ran unhinged as my feet enjoyed the feeling of the grass. I was trying to look out into the woods, but nothing could be seen. It wasn't pitch black, but even if something was out there, my eyes wouldn't be able to make it out. There was no movement around me. No one else seemed to be in their backyards, investigating the noise. Maybe it was all just electrical?

No, I've heard a transformer go out before. Definitely didn't sound like that.

Stepping ahead a little further, I was finally given a vague answer to what might have happened.

At the fence line by the woods, there was a grouping of feathers. Some of them were on the ground, while the rest were stuck to the fence. Blood was also spattered on the fence, but it dripped down into the grass. No body, but I put it together.

"Shit, did a coyote grab one of you?"

I turned to the chicken coop, and they cautiously left their hut. There were now only four of them. But if a coyote got one Thursday night, they did it before it was dark outside, and they got a way cleaner kill. Something seemed off. The two incidents only seemed related in the respect that a chicken was kidnapped or killed. But as for who or what did it...

Was someone screwing with me? If so, they can make a pretty terrifying scream. Maybe it was the kid from the other day. He did say, "New is good." Did that mean he knew I wouldn't know about him taking chickens?

Maybe I could talk to his parents tomorrow. But for now, I headed back inside so I could clean up the bloody mess inside. Upon reentry, Mr. Pickles checked on me. I told him sorry ten times over as I took the bloody washcloth off my hand and placed it in the sink. My hand had stopped bleeding, but previously, it had been bleeding like I had been attacked by a mountain lion. Checking under the sink, I found some pet stain remover, along with different bleaches.

"I don't think Aunt Misty would want me to bleach her rug."

Thinking back to last night's shower, I remembered seeing some band-aids and some peroxide. I figured that would work to get the stains out. So, I made my way to the guest bathroom, and ta-dah, there it was. I'd worry about bandaging my hand later. The sooner I could get the blood out of their furniture, the better. With some peroxide, I wanted to get to work in the living room, but I needed to grab another rag. I jogged back to the kitchen and up to the sink.

"Oh, there's a clean one here in the sink."

Hold on a second...

The same black and white dishrag that I had just used to cover my hand a few minutes ago was now black and white again. To be sure, I lifted it from the sink and flattened it on the counter. Not a single drop of my blood was visible on this previously bloodied rag. I shook my head. This didn't make any sense. Maybe it was one of those new water-repellent rags? Or something? Or did I throw the bloody one away on accident and my memory is messing with me?

Sure, whatever, that would have to make sense for now. I took the rag and moved to the living room. I stepped up to where the incident occurred, ready to prove boys could clean, but again, none of my blood was visible on anything in the living room. The rug, the couch, and even my pants, where some may have dripped, were all clean as could be.

"What the hell... This doesn't make any damn sense."

I promise this isn't hyperbole, but I probably checked the couch and the kitchen sink up and down for an hour or two before finally deciding that I had no reason to continue looking for my own blood. I felt insane. The injury was still on my hand, but all the stains were completely gone. Unless Mr. Pickles was a vampiric cat, I had no explanation for what happened that Friday night. But in the coming days, I'd have way too many answers.

CHAPTER EIGHT

All Eyes on Me

Even though I slept in a real bed this time, the quality of my sleep left much to be desired. Mainly because I couldn't stop thinking about the blood stains, or lack thereof. I was questioning my sanity, but I knew I wasn't imagining things. Mr. Pickles did scratch the hell out of my hand. My hand still wore the scratches like a battle scar. But my own blood just—disappeared. It wasn't on my clothes, or on the couch, or on the wooden floor, or on the living room rug. Not a single drop was in sight, and I was at a loss. Even when I woke up Saturday morning, I was compelled to check around at least one more time while I brewed a pot of coffee.

After being on all fours to check the rug, there was no use. I had to give it up. I wondered if there was a gas leak in the house that was causing me to hallucinate. For some reason, I was only a little disappointed when I didn't blow up the house with my lighter. I didn't smoke, but carrying around a lighter and a pocket knife wasn't unheard of for a "country" kid like myself.

Extremely unsatisfied with way more questions than answers, I decided to look around in Uncle Bob's garage. Surely, something there would interest me or help me get my mind off of things.

There was quite a drop from the kitchen floor to the garage, but a step had been added to make the decline not as drastic. Otherwise, I could imagine my Aunt Misty would have a great fall every day of the week. Closing the door behind me, I flicked the light switches up and barely illuminated the garage. As usual, comparing this house to the previous one really amplified how dissimilar they were from one another. The previous house had a detached garage with boxes stacked to the ceiling. This garage, however, only had one stack of maybe five boxes in an incomplete pyramid, while the rest seemed fairly clean. Lots of tools, manual and power, were hanging from the wall directly ahead of me. There was plenty of room to fit two cars in here, but neither car was here. Surely, they didn't take two cars for their trip.

But there was a beautiful secret under a tarp diagonal from me, and I smiled, feeling pretty sure I knew what it was. Acting like I was in some movie making a big reveal, I yanked the tarp away and revealed the opposite of what I was hoping for.

Instead of my grandpa's awesome Indian motorcycle, it was my grandpa's formerly awesome Indian motorcycle. It didn't appear to have been in a wreck, but the gas tank and engine were missing. Wanting to beat my uncle, I stomped around, hoping to find them nearby. But with my furious footsteps came the discovery of something else. As I approached the garage door, I lost my footing and fell forward. My arms weren't happy with me as I used them to break my fall, but I wasn't quick enough to catch myself with my hands. That's how kids broke their wrists at the roller rinks.

I cursed at myself but was glad I wasn't on the concrete floor. Instead, I was on some heavy rubber mat that seemed to be giving way to my weight. I rolled off of it, and stood up to get a better look.

Sure enough, a roughly rectangular rubber mat resided over... something? Maybe a door or a latch of some kind. To validate my theory, I tried lifting the mat with one hand. It was floppy and awkward, so I used two hands to lift it and let it fall off to the side, stirring up dust. Now instead of a mat, there was a flat metal door. Kneeling down, I tried moving it, but it wouldn't budge. Seeing the dust on my hand, I decided to brush the door off and revealed a handle that was flush to the door. Pressing on one end, the handle popped out, and I was able to easily turn it 90 degrees, which then allowed me to slide it open. The door disappeared into the floor with a new abyss to explore.

I couldn't make out exactly what was at the bottom, as there were no lights to turn on. Debating on whether or not I should even enter, I saw a flashlight up by Uncle Bob's tools and grabbed it. If there wasn't one so close by, I may have convinced myself to postpone this adventure.

Now that I have a flashlight, what's stopping me?

It was a narrow stairwell. All concrete. And even with the flashlight, I couldn't tell exactly how far down it went. The trip into the unknown didn't give me any warm and fuzzy feelings, though. Instead, the musky smell and dingy steps made me uneasy. As I reached the bottom, I looked back to see I was about 15 or 20 feet into the ground. Caverns and caves excited me. This, not so much.

But when the stairs stopped, and the floor was flat once more, I turned left to face a sizable metal door. Similar to the one I entered at the top, the handle was flush to the door, and I had to pop it out to open it. Holding my hand on the handle, I debated on opening it.

"Please don't be some kind of sex dungeon, that's all I ask."

Hoping my prayer was heard, I pulled the handle, and the door rolled quickly open, just to disappear into the wall with a thunderous clang as it stopped. Stepping into the room, I found a light switch on my left and flicked it up. The loud fluorescents crackled above me to shed some light on what existed beneath my uncle's house. I was happy to find out, it wasn't a sex dungeon. It was a doomsday basement.

The room was about the same size as their living room, but the outer walls were shelves upon shelves of perishable goods, supplies, first aid, radios, appliances, and walkie-talkies. On the other end of the room, there was a couch against the wall with a few love seats around a coffee table. A deck of cards was strewn across the table, with half of a bottled water going to waste. I figured my uncle might disappear down here sometimes, but it was more than a man cave. Not to my surprise, there was an extra gun safe, but it appeared to be more secure than the one in their bedroom.

"How the hell did they get everything down here?" I asked, not expecting an answer.

"Meow."

"God!"

I was more afraid than I should have been, but Mr. Pickles sure knew how to pick his moments. I turned to face him, but he was already pressing up against my legs. I turned the flashlight off and rubbed him with it, and the purring ensued.

"Why didn't you tell me about this?"

I wondered if he was even allowed down here. Hell, I probably wasn't allowed, either. And as cool as it was, it got me thinking. The move to a new house, the guns, an underground bunker. Tensions were high in the geopolitical spectrum, but I didn't think Oklahomans needed to worry much about it.

Are they needing all this protection from something else?

My thoughts raced, but Mr. Pickles became focused on something as he began to growl. He let out a long cry that wavered in pitch and intensity. The sound you hear right before two alley cats beat the crap out of each other.

"What is it?"

He was low to the ground with his tail whipping sporadically. He had his eyes on something near the couch and loveseats, but I couldn't quite make it out. Even with my approach, Mr. Pickles stayed in position, and I could tell he was shaking. But even after stepping up to him to see what he was looking at, I didn't know what to think.

It was a little red pool that was in sort of a disk shape, but the liquid had waves to it. The sheen made it look waxy, and as I watched it flow in a contained shape, a drop of the red liquid fell from the ceiling. My head jerked up and all I saw was a circular red stain that was slowly becoming smaller. The liquid only dripped from the center of the mass, and fell directly into the frisbee of... my blood?

Mr. Pickles was done staring at it. After a few more drips, he shrieked, jumped back, and ran back up into the main house. I, on the other hand, wasn't sure what to do. But if it was my blood, it didn't look like blood anymore. It was thickening, but maintaining the same shape. It wasn't increasing in size, even though the stain above was slowly shrinking. I think a normal person may have left well enough alone, but for whatever reason, I felt drawn to it. I wanted to touch it and see what would happen.

Trying to be braver than the cat, I got down on all fours and started to reach out. But as my fingers inched closer, a faint ringing was heard in my right ear. It started there, then went to my left ear, and then both began ringing louder than anything I had ever heard. I didn't stop reaching for it, though. I pressed on, determined to make contact. It wasn't until I was a few inches away that the disk of blood finally changed shape, and dented inward, away from my fingers. The ringing became muffled, but it was still there. My eyes started to water. Maybe this wasn't a good idea. My dumbass kept trying to touch it, even if I could only poke it for a second. It just made sense to me.

Bad news, the script finally flipped. And when my fingers began entering the concave section of the disk, it formed back into its original shape and my fingers were now stuck in the blob. In an instant, I went from my ears ringing at full blast to losing all feeling in my arm. Excruciating chest pains slammed me repeatedly, and I cried out in pain. The room felt like it was vibrating, and my vision went black.

* * *

"Hey, you okay?"

I woke up slowly, but my vision wouldn't focus. When it finally did, I found the mailman hovering over me.

"Huh? How did you get in here?"

Unassumingly, the mailman replied, "Well, the garage door was wide open. Then I saw the hatch was ajar and figured you might be down here."

"Alright."

Remembering what had transpired, I sat up quickly and looked around. There was no blood stain on the ceiling. No disk of blood on the ground. But when I looked at my right hand, the three scratch marks had blackened instead of being red like before.

"Did you get a tattoo or something?"

"No," I replied. "But, did you know about this?"

"About what? The shelter? Yeah. The neighbors actually all worked together to pay for it. They convinced your uncle before they built their house. In fact, I remember these cooky neighbors of yours were digging around this house, even before it was built."

"Digging?"

"Yeah, the whole lot of them. They didn't get far, though. Hit a lot of clay. Guess it was a way for them to work out or something."

"Why would they have this built?"

The mailman reached down and lifted me off the ground. I thanked him as we stood face-to-face.

"I suppose it's since none of the other houses have a proper storm shelter. Well, except Dr. Montgomery on the other side of the neighborhood."

"A doctor lives here?"

"Former college professor. Pretty neat guy. I like your uncle, too, though. He let me come down here a few times."

"Neat," I said plainly.

I wanted to ask more questions, but I started putting a few pieces together of my own. The blob. My hand. The scratches...

"Oh crap, Mr. Pickles!"

"Hey, he isn't supposed to be outside now, is he? I think I saw him down the street."

"Great, thanks," I replied, and I ran out of the garage.

The mailman yelled something about signing the package for me, and I waved. Keeping a good pace, my eyes scanned each house as I passed it. Kids and parents were standing around outside, playing and talking. They took turns glaring at me, but I didn't care to interact with anyone. I trusted the mailman, and sure enough, after passing the second house on the north side, I found Mr. Pickles approaching the middle house. I stopped running once I reached their mailbox, and had to take a few breaths. Immediately, something seemed different about this house. Where all the other houses were lively with kids, this one appeared to have none. For some reason, I was bothered that their lights were off. It was around 1pm so the sun was doing its job, but it was odd to not see a single light on inside. Or maybe it was strange that not a single window had blinds. They did appear to be closed, but they were pristinely clean, so it was easy to look right in. My parents taught me not to stare, but no one had taught Mr. Pickles.

Not my smartest move, but I tried running to Mr. Pickles and he bolted to the right side of the house. Now remembering the term "scaredy cat," I slowed my approach from behind as he continued walking. He was going into their backyard, and I looked to see if the owner would mind. The house looked dead, so I continued to follow Mr. Pickles into their unfenced backyard. My eyes stayed down as I watched him saunter forward.

"Glad he didn't go into those trees on the left side," I muttered.

But when I stepped from green grass to tan gravel, I looked up and regretted it.

In the backyard of the quiet house was the church from the pamphlet. The Church of New Beginnings. It even said so on a small sign by the front door. It was a narrow building that fit directly behind the two-story house. Seeing it in person, I realized how accurate the pamphlet was. The church probably wasn't up to code, but it might safely fit about 50 people, at a glance. I couldn't tell if the dark exterior was caused by nature or man. Either way, it wasn't the prettiest thing to look at. Mr. Pickles seemed to share my sentiment but took it a step further when he stopped in place and hissed at the building. Then, he started acting the same way as he had down in the basement. My memories were fully coming back, and I looked down at my hand.

"The church called to you."

My gut told me not to turn around, but my brain went for it out of curiosity. The booming voice belonged to a man much taller than me, with long, sleek black hair and a well-groomed, flat black beard. I was barely six feet tall, but this guy had to be around 6'5". He wore almost entirely all black, along with a pilgrim-era hat. I wanted to ask him if he was looking for his time machine, but his blank stare pierced through any jokes I may have had. Not to mention the phrase he used to make himself known.

"Called for me? Oh, I was just looking for my cat," I replied dumbly.

Keeping the stoic look, he coldly replied, "How have you been?"

He stared, waiting for an answer that I didn't have. As nicely as I could, I said, "Uh, have we met before?"

For the first time, the man blinked and then took a step back from me. His face changed from blank to friendly, and he replied, "Oh, I guess we haven't. I'm Pastor Blackwood. Do you live around here?"

The lack of questions revolving around me being behind his house surprised me, but the friendlier he wanted to be, the better.

"Yeah, I'm watching my aunt and uncle's house," I said, pointing in the general direction. "Their cat got out, and I was trying to find him when I saw him entering your backyard. Sorry for trespassing."

His smile didn't match the rest of his body language as he replied, "No, no, that's okay. Animals are important."

"Yeah, my aunt would not be pleased if he went missing."

Mr. Pickles seemed to break his focus away from the church as I lifted him up, holding his legs with my right hand. Instead of fussing, he seemed to fall asleep in my arms, exhausted from the adventure.

Holding him made me feel a bit safer, but now I needed to get back home.

"Cats," Pastor Blackwood said with a hiss at the end. "Hmph. What was your name?"

"I'm Chris."

The pastor reached out to shake my hand, but I gestured towards the cat with my chin.

"Ah, it would be hard to shake hands now. Right. Tell me, Chris, what do you think of my church?"

I couldn't decide if I should be honest or a liar. I decided to mix both into a pot and reply, "It looks great. Really stands out now that I'm back here looking at it. It's pretty hidden away otherwise, but I got a flyer from the mailman about the place."

"Oh? Well, now, that flyer was for him, not for others."

"Hey, I'm sure he meant no offense. In fact, at this point, I'm pretty much a collector of your pamphlets. The owner of the gas station outside of town gave me one, too."

"Is that so?" Pastor Blackwood replied. It seemed as though telling him that the flyers were being passed along like recycling really peeved him.

"Yeah but, oh well, right? Their loss."

His smile returned, and he replied, "That's a great point, Chris. Their loss, your gain. Maybe the church called to you after all. Tomorrow at 11am is our next gathering. Might you join?"

"Tomorrow at 11am? Uh, sure, I don't think I have anything else going on around then. I was curious, though, what denomination are y'all?"

"Denomination? Hmm. What denomination are you now?"

"I'd say... Catholic? Sort of."

"Doesn't sound like you truly belong anywhere, then. You'd be perfect for our group."

"Well, I am from out of town, so I don't know if I can continue going here after the first time. I'm just watching my aunt and uncle's house."

"We'd still love to have you."

Mr. Pickles woke up from his slumber and shifted around in my arms. He was becoming a bit more difficult to hold, and the pastor took note of it.

"How about you hop in my Mule, and I'll drive you home? I'm sure you don't want to carry him all the way back."

My arms were already feeling a bit sore from holding the 13-pound fur baby, so I nodded, and Pastor Blackwood went to the other side of his house to fetch the vehicle. I hadn't heard of one before, but when he pulled up to me, I saw it was just an upgraded ATV with a front and back seating area, along with a small flatbed. It seemed like it would be good for hauling hay, but I didn't see any around. Or, it was good for taking your neighbor home after chasing down a cat.

I started to climb into the back but Pastor Blackwood insisted I ride in the front. No sense in arguing, I got in the front seat and he drove out onto the main street. Again, the families from the houses around us gave me a look, but it wasn't as disapproving as last time. Sometimes, the pastor would nod his head slowly or give a little wave, but he was back to an indifferent stare.

"Does everyone in this neighborhood attend your church?" I asked.

"Yes, mostly."

"Must be nice to have a church like this right in the neighborhood. Almost like you all are family."

He grinned and nodded. Before I could even give any directions, he pulled up to my uncle's house.

"Chris, I'm glad you found the cat, and I do hope you join us tomorrow."

A bit hesitant, I turned and asked, "How'd you know which house I was watching?"

"Well, you told me," he replied slyly. "You pointed, said your cat got out, and that you were watching Uncle Robert and Aunt Misty's house."

Saying that I called him Uncle Robert really solidified that I hadn't told him any of what he was saying. Or maybe he was friends with my uncle and knew they were going out of town. But does Pastor Blackwood actually keep tabs on all the people in the neighborhood? It wouldn't be out of the question if everyone attended the same church.

"Did you have any more questions, child?" Pastor Blackwood asked.

"Hey, I resent that. I'm 18, after all," I said, trying to lighten the mood. "No, but thank you for the ride."

"You're welcome, Chris. And I'll see you at 11 tomorrow morning."

CHAPTER NINE

The Church of Infamy

Another basketball game was on, so that's how I wasted my Saturday night. And luckily, I didn't hear anything out of the ordinary. Mr. Pickles didn't scratch me. The flow of electricity throughout the house stayed consistent. Dare I say, it was a normal night. The only odd thing that stayed as proof of the weirdness was the blackened scratches on the back of my hand. Mr. Pickles had apologized a few times over with cuddles and purring, and I had long forgiven him. Trying to go to bed Saturday night, I could still remember the shriek I had heard in the backyard. Was it one of the chickens crying out? No clue.

But for the first time in what felt like a long time, I woke up to get cleaned up and ready for church.

My aunt and uncle had plenty of clothes to choose from, but I figured it'd be best to stick to my uncle's attire. He had plenty of suit coats, ironed shirts, slacks, and shoes. Unfortunately, the shoes didn't fit me, so I would have to wear one of his suits with my sneakers. As I passed by the mirror, I saw that it wouldn't hurt me to shave my face. My facial hair grew in patchy, never consistent. And it seemed to have grown in overnight. Feeling like a mooch, I found the newest-looking disposable razor and an aerosol can of shaving cream, so I could get to work.

Once I looked smooth enough, I used some aftershave and then hopped in the shower. I probably wasn't following the correct order of operations, but it'd have to do for now. After the shower, my face felt a bit rough and looked unhappy with redness. Ignoring it, I swiped on deodorant, sprayed a terrible cologne followed by a decent one, and walked out to their bedroom from the master bathroom.

I placed my clothes on the bed before the shower, and of course, Mr. Pickles curled up on top of the pants. I tried to slowly pick up the pants, but he responded quicker when I yanked them.

"Sorry, pal. I guess if you escape again, you know where the church is."

If I can say so myself, I dressed pretty well. I even found a nice watch to add to the outfit. Only thing missing was a tie, since I couldn't remember how to tie one. After only fumbling with it for a bit, I stuffed it in my coat pocket and went to the kitchen.

Three chickens greeted me from the backyard as I poured myself a glass of water from the kitchen sink. The sun was beating down more than the last few melancholy days, and with the minimal wind, I opened the window to let some fresh air into the house. Checking the fridge, I found a fruit basket and nabbed an apple. Standing in their kitchen, dressed to the nines, eating an apple, I thought about how old I must have looked. What's next, do I read the newspaper?

There was indeed a newspaper on the kitchen table, and another one by their kitchen phone. My aunt and uncle didn't have an answering machine, so I wasn't sure if they had called. But I was spending most of my time at their house, so I would have heard the phone by now. Well, unless it rang while I reached out to... whatever that was in the basement.

Having a hard time remembering what I did after saving Mr. Pickles, I opened the garage door and poked my head out. The garage door was closed, as was the hatch leading down under. I just needed to place the mat back over it at some point, but that could wait.

Mr. Pickles tried to go out in the garage, but I shooed him back into the house. He wasn't very happy with me today. First, no morning cuddles, then the pants, and now this.

"When I get home, we can watch golf or something. That'll put me to sleep."

"Ray-ow."

He pouted and stormed off to the living room. Offering to go ahead and turn on the TV for him, the TV clicked and we joined midway into a news story. I faintly heard the anchorman talk about two men going missing in the last five days, but I checked my uncle's watch.

"10:42. Guess I'll go ahead and get to walking."

I approached the front door, making sure I had everything I needed. Wondering if there would be a collection plate, I checked my wallet. I had loose change I could spare, or a dollar as a courtesy, anyway. I wasn't trying to score a gold membership or anything.

Putting my wallet away, I brushed myself off and sighed. I wasn't excited or nervous about church. Going alone would be odd, but who else was I supposed to bring?

Finally, I reached out to the front door and looked down. Of course, I was drawn to my injury and how the scratch marks had puffed up and turned black. They almost looked like tar, and I was bad about scratching at my scabs. But these would not come off. It didn't really hurt to poke at them, they just felt stuck.

For some reason, while looking at my hand, I noticed the extra pamphlet on the entry table, along with the revolver I had answered the door with. Talk about a lack of gun safety on my part.

"I don't think I need a gun for church, but I should put it up when I get back."

But something about the pamphlet was making my paranoia go berserk. Didn't the pamphlet mention that they're an army? Or to join their army? Yesterday, Pastor Blackwood simply called them a group. But if I rejected their group, would they retaliate?

"C'mon, it's a church. Not a cult. Leave the gun. Take the cannoli."

I didn't feel comfortable running in the suit, so walking would have to do. I wasn't the only one. Like clockwork, I watched as each and every house in the neighborhood emptied with perfectly quaint and well-dressed families. The kids bounced with each step. The mothers were smiling while the fathers scolded the kids for being too fast. Everyone seemed to have left in sync. Pastor Blackwood had cast a wide net, and not a single neighbor wiggled loose.

"The new one is going to join us."

Turning to my right, I saw the family next door walking past my uncle's house. The speaker was the little boy who stared at me over the fence for so long my first night here. He kept his left arm stretched out with his index finger pointing at me. He was maybe seven years old, while his sister looked about ten. The mother reached out to lower her son's hand and said, "That would be great if you would join us. I know your aunt and uncle would like that."

Okay, I know I've thought it over before, but the fact that everyone in the damn neighborhood knew about my aunt and uncle going out of town and their nephew watching their house was really unnerving to me. I guessed they were all trying to be nice, but it didn't seem like Uncle Bob to tell everyone so openly about going out of town. In retrospect, he didn't even tell my parents about moving houses, as far as I knew. I figured my mom would have told me. She tells me everything. Like when she told me that Becky at the casino wears a size seven and likes Little River Band. Why would she tell me that but not that her brother moved houses?

Trying to convince myself not to overanalyze every single little thing, I waved and then followed behind them. Everyone was dressed nice. The sun was out. Everyone was smiling. What did I have to be worried about?

I couldn't hear what the parents were talking about in front of me, but their two kids took turns looking back at me. I tried smiling and waving each time, but it got tiresome after a while. Besides, they weren't smiling and waving back at me, so fuck them.

I didn't have tracks to prove it, but something told me we were walking the exact same path Mr. Pickles had yesterday. As everyone closed in on the Pastor's house, they walked around to the east side of the yard, just as I had the day before. No one entered his backyard from the west due to a collection of trees and tall grass. I wanted to just spite everyone, but figured it was best to go with the flow.

Compared to most of the rest of the neighbors entering the church, I appeared to stand out. I hadn't impregnated anyone yet, or gotten married, therefore, I was an outcast. But Pastor Blackwood and the woman I assumed was his wife stood at the entryway of the church, shaking hands and granting blessings to all those who were attending. They didn't appear to have children. Or if they did, they were nowhere in sight. Pastor Blackwood was wearing the same outfit, more or less, while his wife wore a muted cream-colored floral dress. The dress looked stiff and old, while she looked maybe five or six years north of my age. Pastor Blackwood was probably in his 40s, and I felt like a sideshow act trying to guess ages.

Continuing my trend, the kids that frolicked about appeared to all be pre-teens. There were a few other young men about, maybe in their mid-to late-20s. They wore button-up shirts and slacks, but I was the only one with a suit coat on. Well, until I saw the other outcast.

A man in his late 50s stood by a tree, with a young lady that looked to be around my age. The man had strong, long brown hair down to his shoulder blades. He wore a nice brown peacoat with a brown shirt underneath, along with, well, surprise, brown slacks and brown shoes. His ovular glasses caught my attention as the sun bounced off of them. He was speaking to the young lady, who had her dark hair in a tight bun, along with a woman's suit and white flats. She sported a small purse that didn't look big enough to even fit anything in it, but what did I know. Neither of them smiled, nor did they look bewildered.

While I was so tired of people staring at me, I couldn't help but stare at them. The longer I did, the more I realized how much they stood out compared to everyone else I had walked by. I hoped they weren't a couple because of the age gap, so I assumed he was her father or grandfather. Everyone else here was husband, wife, and two or three kids. Multiply that by 18 houses, and that's… an army.

The crowd outside of the church started to thin, but I kept staring. Finally, the young lady whispered something to the man, and he looked right at me. I could see the gears turning in his head as he looked me up and down, but I had no idea what the output was. Were they even going to go inside the church?

"Chris, child."

I reluctantly stopped staring at them and turned to the stupid pastor. His arms were up and out as if he was going to catch an angel.

"Remember, I'm 18," I replied.

"You didn't meet my partner," he said, ignoring my comment. "Madeline, this is Chris. He's watching Robert and Misty's house."

"How wonderful for you to join us," she said. "Come on inside, we won't bite."

I didn't find her statement reassuring, but I did as she asked and made my way inside. As dingy as it was on the outside, the inside was warm and clean. The lighting worked, but I didn't see any windows. Once I was inside, I had no idea what it looked like outside anymore. It felt like time could move pretty fast in their church.

Upon entering, I noticed a stairwell to my left. An organ was playing from above, and the song didn't sound familiar to me at all. Not all churches played the same songs, but the song that was playing didn't seem very uplifting. If this was actually a funeral, I must have been the last one to find out.

There were candles on the walls above each set of pews. Someone in white, gold, and red robes was finishing their task of lighting them all with an ornate curved cane. He still had candles to light at the front, by the wood podium, and I faintly caught a glimpse of his face as he turned. If he was only in white robes and had a white hood, I definitely would have turned around and left.

Kids were still fussing about. The adults were either leaning over pews, talking to each other, or embracing, or on their knees praying. The lighting, colors, and people made me think of Catholic church, but there was one thing that I didn't realize until I sat down.

If these people were Christian, there was no imagery of Jesus. Or God. The Heavens. Nothing. The walls were mostly plain, and even when I sat down in the pew, I didn't find any kind of Bible waiting for me. Or a hymn book. Although, no one else was trying to sing along to the organ player, so I didn't figure I should try either.

I sat somewhere in the middle and to the right. The kids were mostly in the front rows, with the men and women in their 20s scattered between them. I guessed they were the babysitters, while I was sitting by several older parents. No one else was in my row, but I liked it that way. I should have known this place wouldn't have A/C, but damn. After only a few minutes of being seated, I was getting drenched with sweat. It was either take the coat off and expose my embarrassing sweat stains, or endure.

The front door abrasively swung closed. The sound echoed, and the kids started to finally shut up. My neck twisted so my eyes could see what was going on. Pastor Blackwood and Madeline made their way to the front of the church, but behind them were the man and lady from the tree. I watched as they sat in a row near the exit, but the man's look at me this time was a bit more comforting. I faced the front and watched Pastor Blackwood kiss Madeline on the forehead for an awkwardly long time. Finally, the organ player decided to take a break, and Pastor Blackwood's boots clomped onto the front stage. The organ player came down the stairs and paced to a seat behind Pastor Blackwood. He wore the same kind of robes as the candle lighter, who ended up sitting next to the organ player. Once they were quietly seated, Pastor Blackwood opened up a book on the podium and started.

"Hello, family. I know it has only been a week since our last convene, but my, I've missed you all. How are we?"

I shrugged, but the rest of the attendants said in near perfect unison, "Ready for the beginning."

"Yes, the new beginning. That's what we're all looking forward to. And with new beginnings…"

"… come new challenges," the group replied.

"Yes. But these challenges can be faced and overcome. Especially if we're all together."

"Strength in numbers, just as It would want," they replied again.

"Hey, uh, excuse me."

The fact that I spoke seemed to outrage some and confuse others. I went ahead and stood up too, just so everyone knew which asshole talked.

"No, don't be alarmed, family. This is Child Chris. Shares ancestry with Robert and Misty," Pastor Blackwood answered.

"Yeah, they're my aunt and uncle. Anyway, I don't mean to interrupt, but do you have a script or something, so I can follow along with how to respond."

"Hah!" Pastor Blackwood cried. "A script? No, there is no script. Just sit and listen, Chris, and you will know the answers for next time."

Everyone, and I mean everyone, was staring at me. For good reason, I suppose. Pastor Blackwood seemed like the kind of man who had never been interrupted in his life. And I could already tell, based on what little I had seen so far, that he loved the sound of his own voice. I also wanted to clarify that I wouldn't be coming back, but I left well enough alone and sat back down.

"Now, family, as you all see, we have new guests. Not just Chris, but Dr. Montgomery and his granddaughter Lisa have joined us for the first time as well. And at such a pinnacle in time."

The attendants gave off a soft laugh. Maybe I should have left as soon as I heard the shitty organ player.

"The time is near. We have all felt it, haven't we?"

"The shakes, the rumble, as you foretold."

The shakes, the rumble? Do they mean Friday night?

"It will rise once again. It wants to. But there's a price to be paid."

"The sacrifices of our blood."

"Oh, so are you guys talking about like, the second coming of Christ and all?"

I was standing once again with another burning question, but the organ player didn't take too kindly to it.

"Shut up, with your bastard blood! No one speaks over the Pastor."

He was red in the face and spit way too much during his spat. He shook with a tremendous amount of rage as he pointed me down. I wanted to laugh but feared what he would do after. Plus, no one else in the church found it funny.

"Thomas, rest," Pastor Blackwood commanded softly. "Child Chris is confused. He's a lost soul, just like so many of you were. He doesn't belong anywhere. I can sense uncertainty in your future, Chris."

"So, are we not talking about Jesus Christ? You mentioned the second coming. I thought that was all about…"

"The second coming? No. No, what we speak of has nothing to do with that fairytale."

"Yikes," I blurted, even though I wasn't very religious. But saying something like that in my hometown could get someone killed.

"I understand. You're stuck on a story that's become commonplace. Why wouldn't you believe it? But what if I were to tell you that there's a greater being? One that was betrayed 200 years ago instead of 2000?"

"Pastor, he doesn't even know our story, and he doesn't have enough respect to listen," the organ player complained.

"Now, Thomas, I feel you are the one interjecting."

Looking defeated, the organ player sat down. I remained

standing, but my legs started to feel weak. What the hell were they talking about?

"Look, I apologize."

"Your apology is unnecessary. Virgins always have the most questions," Pastor Blackwood stated as he turned an eye to Madeline, who weirdly enough smiled at the comment.

"Uh, yeah. Okay. I'll just sit down now."

"Chris, child, it is refreshing to have such curiosity. But allow me to finish the planned sermon before we discuss things further, okay? You may have an important role in the new beginning."

Due to popular demand, I sat down and told myself to keep my mouth shut. It relieved the rest of the neighborhood as they turned to face the pastor once more.

"Our story is a long one, but it's definitely worth your time. I think it will enlighten you and give you a purpose in life that you never imagined. We are all soldiers, after all, as everyone else knows. But before the new beginning occurs and the war begins, we must make sure we are all prepared for the sacrifice that will be asked of us. You all do understand, correct?"

"Yes, Pastor."

"Good. And remember that when the time comes, hesitation will not be an option."

"For the good of our congregation. For a future so rich."

"Let us pray."

Out of respect, I followed everyone and bowed my head. I didn't know what we were supposed to pray for, but I prayed that I could get the hell out of this church soon. My prayer was answered, but not in the way I expected.

What started as silent prayer became an ever-growing chant. It wasn't a language I felt like I had ever heard, but before I knew it, my mouth was trying to move with the sounds. On top of that, my hand started to burn. Yeah, that hand. Breaking my concentration, my fingers jerked around like never before as my right arm spasmed. The joints were even popping as they flailed in absolutely unnatural ways. Even worse, the black lines appeared to move and flow, and a burning sensation accompanied it. I started thinking back to when I was in the basement, and I came in contact with my blood. It wasn't burning as bad as that, but it was intensifying. I tried my best to hold it together, but as their chanting got louder, my ears started to ring. A migraine hit me, and my vision started getting hazy. I wanted to stay in my seat, but doing so any longer would be torture.

Everyone still had their heads down as I made my way out of the pew. Holding my right hand in agony, I made my way to the door. The only ones that didn't have their heads down were the man and the young lady. Only glancing at them for a second, I heard the pastor call out, "Wait, Child Chris!"

I burst through the door and alerted the congregation. Glad I was wearing sneakers and not dress shoes, I made a run for it. The farther away the church became, the better I felt. I didn't know what it was about the chant that upset me, but nearing my uncle's was a relief. I should have known better, but I looked back. The entire neighborhood was watching me run from the pastor's house. I thought I would be terrified if I saw them chasing after me, but it was even more unsettling to watch them turn around and storm the pastor's home, like they were running a drill they had practiced for years.

It didn't matter. I got into my uncle's house, locked every door leading outside, and grabbed the 10-gauge shotgun. It was loaded to the brim with shells, and I wasn't afraid to use it. Something was very wrong about these people, I just didn't quite know what.

Mr. Pickles was on edge as soon as I entered, and I didn't have the strength to tell him not to worry. I didn't know if it was better to lock myself in the house, or down in the basement. But I didn't want to have an episode in the basement again.

I was huffing and puffing, enough to blow a little pig's house down. This was insane. It was all insane. A being greater than Christ that died 200 years ago? That rang zero bells to me.

I was getting lightheaded. I had to sit down. But before I could choose where to sit, I fell against the wall with no strength and slid to the floor.

CHAPTER TEN

Second Worst Night of My Life

"**C**hris?"

My eyelids flickered, but I couldn't quite wake up. "Chris?"

It was a woman's voice, but I couldn't snap out of it. My body wasn't responding to my brain's commands. Trying again, I opened my eyes and saw the shotgun in my arms. Shaking my head, I looked up and screamed.

"Chris, child?"

Madeline and Pastor Blackwood took turns putting their heads in the side window of the front door to look in at me. Their smiles were empty. I stood up, holding the shotgun against me and not sure where to aim, and it was then I realized that I had summoned a mob.

The entire neighborhood stood out in the front yard, some carrying torches, some just clapping and smiling. The kids ran around aimlessly, but they were all gathered on the front lawn of my uncle's house. Looking at the backyard, I wasn't completely surrounded. But I wasn't going to go running into the woods.

"Chris, come out. Please. We'd love to tell you your role in all of this."

Realizing it probably wasn't best to run outside and gun down an entire neighborhood, I shook my head and yelled, "I'm calling the police!"

No one was trying to force their way in, but as I made my way to the kitchen, I saw someone heading for the kitchen window.

That's right! I left it open!

Now with more of a spring in my step, I ran and closed the window, locking it tight. The man who tried to make an approach smiled and continued staring at me, muttering words to himself that I couldn't understand. I didn't want to understand. And the longer he stood there, the more people started gathering in the backyard, peering through every window of my uncle's house.

Trembling in fear, I yanked the kitchen landline up to my ear and called the police. Everyone in the backyard seemed unphased. They continued taking turns staring in and talking to each other, each seeming as jolly as the next person. After three rings, a woman answered, "9-1-1, what is your emergency?"

"Hello, I'm Chris, I'm watching my aunt and uncle's house, and I have a mob outside the house."

"A mob? Are you in danger?"

"Yes, they're at the front door and back door."

"Do you know these people? Are they trying to enter the house?"

"It's some church group. I'm out in Ruby Falls. Please, just send a SWAT team or something!"

"Calm down, sir. Are they trying to enter the house?"

I listened and didn't hear any glass breaking or anyone trying to open doors. I figured they had already tried a clean entry when I was asleep. Now, they just watched me squirm with happiness plastered on their faces. They appeared lucid beyond possibility.

"No, I don't think so. But they're surrounding the house."

"Chris, child, please come out. We only wish to speak with you," Pastor Blackwood called from the front door.

"Yes, please come out," they all said, overlapping each other, the voices becoming thunderous.

"Is that them I hear in the background?" the dispatcher replied.

"Yes. It's the entire neighborhood or church or whatever you want to call them," I answered, while my feelings moved from fear to anger.

"Sounds like they just want you to join their activities. Why did you call us again?"

"Are you fucking serious?" I replied, watching them peer in. "No, this isn't a friendly group. They have torches, for Christ's sake."

"Well, it is dark outside."

"Is this call being recorded?" I yelled. "If so, send a fucking car, now!"

"Chris, is everything alright? There's no need to yell," Pastor Blackwood reassured.

"Yeah, yeah, shut the fuck up and go away! All of you!"

"Sir, I can stay on the line, but I'm going to need you to calm down," the dispatcher advised.

"I just, I don't know what to do. They're not coming in, but they're staring me down. They won't leave unless I go outside, and I don't know what they'll do once I go outside."

"Are you armed?" the dispatcher asked.

"Yes, I have my uncle's shotgun with me."

"Then I would advise if you do go outside, to go unarmed. Otherwise, you will be seen as the aggressor."

"Dammit," I said.

There was no way I was going outside, but if I didn't, would these people ever go away? Would they stay peaceful, or would they eventually get hostile? That was the part I didn't want to wait around for and find out. I just wanted a police officer or a SWAT team to come out and disperse the crowd. Make them leave and never come back.

Eventually, as I breathed heavily into the phone, I heard Pastor Blackwood issue an ultimatum.

"Child Chris, I want you to listen very carefully before you answer my question. If you do not wish to come out and be amongst us, are you saying you deny the existence of our leader? You deny our cause?"

Part of me wanted to ask him to elaborate on what the hell their cause actually was, but the majority of me wanted this all to be over as soon as possible. So, without thinking too much about it, I blurted out, "I deny it. I deny everything!"

With my declaration, all the smiley faces watching me died, and everyone now looked like they hadn't had their morning coffee in weeks. Dreary and defeated, I heard an exaggerated sigh from Pastor Blackwood as he said, "Foolish child. Family, as much as it pains me, we must leave the non-believers behind. Let us disperse for tonight."

They did as the pastor commanded since his word seemed to be absolute. It still wasn't fast enough, but I was relieved that they were shuffling away. Even as they dispersed, I still felt surrounded. It was the entire neighborhood vs me.

"Sir, are you still there?" the dispatcher asked.

"Yes. I don't believe it, but they're leaving."

"Okay, I'd recommend you disconnect the call if you feel safe now."

"I... I think I'd still like a police car out here first thing in the morning. They said they were done for tonight. Who knows what they plan to do tomorrow."

"Kid, I think it was all a misunderstanding. Get some rest and put the gun down."

"Sure, thanks."

Tired of the condescension, I dropped the phone onto the receiver and ended the call. Not able to completely decompress, I still had to check every single window and door. After the third time patrolling, I went back to the bedroom and found Mr. Pickles on the bed, waiting for the all-clear.

"They're gone, for now."

Placing the shotgun on the bed, I took the suit coat off and unbuttoned the shirt about halfway when I heard a knock at the front door.

"No fucking way."

Grabbing the shotgun once more, I ran out of the bedroom and peeked through the dining room from the hallway. I didn't see a gathering of people, so I eased into the living room to see no one in the backyard, either. Now, I was mad at myself for not closing the blinds. Oh well. I was 100% ready to blast the next person I saw.

Until I realized it was the man from the tree. He stood alone in the same attire as before, so we had that in common. He wasn't holding a torch or begging me to join his cause, so I placed the shotgun down by the entryway table and slightly opened the door.

"Wow, I'm surprised you answered," he said smoothly.

"What do you want?" I asked.

"I'd like to speak with you."

"Are you Dr. Montgomery?"

He smiled and said, "Yes. Can I come in?"

I looked back. Even though my uncle owned enough guns in various places to more than adequately defend himself, I struggled to be friendly after what had just happened.

"No, sorry. I'd really just like to be alone."

"Chris, it's important that I speak with you. I'm even offering that you sleep over at my house, just so you're not alone. What you went through was not normal."

"Yeah, no shit. But I don't know a thing about you, either. So, I think I'll take my chances here."

Dr. Montgomery's eyes twinkled as he sourly replied, "I don't agree, but if you insist. Here, my phone number in case anything comes up. I only sleep about four hours a night, so call me anytime."

He offered up a folded piece of paper, and I nabbed it from him.

"Thanks for your concern. Goodnight."

As much as closing the door in Dr. Montgomery's face seemed to be the right decision at the time, I did feel some regret as he slowly walked away. He seemed like a genuinely nice person who had my best interest in mind, but I wasn't ready to take any more chances. I shouldn't have touched that blob in the basement. I shouldn't have gone to church. Reviewing all my poor decisions made me want to reconsider Dr. Montgomery's offer, but it was too late. No way was I going to walk alone in the dark to get to his house. I didn't even know which one was his.

Lifting the shotgun, I caught a whiff of my terrible body odor from all the sweating in the church. Might sound weird, but the smell excited me. It meant I could take another shower in their awesome master bathroom. Taking all my clothes off as the shower warmed felt like a state of meditation in its own right. I didn't know if I should try washing the suit in their laundry machines or just leave it for when they got back. That's IF they even come back.

Stepping into the shower, I splashed some of the hot water on my body so I could get acclimated. The thought crossed my mind to shower with the shotgun, but it stayed on the bed with Mr. Pickles. We were all exhausted. My brain didn't want to think anymore. But complete relaxation wasn't possible. I'd close my eyes only to see Pastor Blackwood or Madeline or the organ player or the candle lighter staring back at me. Smiling, waving, pleading for me to join them. I actually preferred it when the organ player yelled at me in front of everyone.

Scrubbing down my armpits, I looked at my scratched hand and tried washing off the three black lines. It was no use. They seemed to be here to stay. Did Mr. Pickles have some kind of disease that infected my hand, or was it caused by touching the blob in the basement? The lines only turned black after interacting with the blob, so that made the most sense. But the question still remained, what was that thing?

CLICK!

Suddenly, the power was out, and I was in complete darkness. The water continued running, but that wouldn't help anything. I stepped back, reaching for the towel that I draped over before stepping in. I wondered if there was a short, but I knew I was just trying to be optimistic.

Someone had cut the power intentionally.

I left the water running and wiped myself down quickly. Then, I threw on some pajama pants and peeked out to the bedroom. My eyes were adjusting, but I could see that no one was coming in. The moonlight was helping a bit but left a lot to be desired. Trying to think of the best plan, I decided to stuff some pillows under the comforter on my uncle's side, and then I could hide away on my aunt's side with the shotgun.

Satisfied with the plan, I buried some pillows the best I could on my uncle's side, making it look like someone was in bed. But after I snuck over to my aunt's side, I realized I left the shower water running.

Not sure if it would be helpful or hurtful, well, it couldn't be helped. I could hear footsteps in the hallway. Sounded like two or three people, but I wasn't sure. They sounded excited in their suppressed banter. I tried breathing as quietly as I could, but it was impossible. I peeked over the bed sneakily, only to see beams from flashlights dancing around in the hallway. Whoever it was, they weren't being very covert. They were bold and didn't sound the least bit afraid of me. I was the only one terrified. Then, as one neared the bedroom door, they recited something I had never heard.

"We were deceived, we tried and tried, we all pray for the Gowl-Die."

The what?

"Sounds like he's in the shower."

"Maybe. But don't do it in there."

I only heard two voices, both male. They were entering the bedroom now. The shotgun was ready, but I wasn't. Punching Todd in the face was the most violence I had ever inflicted on someone. The thought of firing a gun at someone made me sick to my stomach, but I remembered what my grandpa had told me about killing Germans in the war.

"I just had to tell myself, it was them or me. Both of us could go home, but one was going in a box."

I didn't even know when to fire. Maybe they were unarmed. Should I just do a warning shot into the ceiling and piss off my uncle?

"Hey," one of them said, now whispering. "I think he's in the bed."

I could hear one of them breathing on the other side of the bed, staring at the pillows. Only one of them had a flashlight, and that person moved to the bathroom to check the shower.

"He ain't in here. Thomas, do it."

Wanting to take revenge, the organ player raised the knife and said, "Please accept the flesh of the non-believer. HA!"

The knife plunged into the bed with a loud thump, but when he tried to bring it back up, he called out, "Damn thing is stuck!"

That's when I decided to act.

I adjusted to where I was on my knees, and I swung the shotgun over the bed. The silhouette of the organ player looked back at me, but I didn't see his facial expression until I fired. The blast from the shotgun revealed his surprised look, but it was too late. Even though I had fired a little too far to the left, half of his face exploded in a red mist of bone and blood while the other half was covered in black gunpowder. He had tried to scream or call out for help, but the screams were interrupted by the blast. His body crumpled, still stuck to the bed as blood gushed out and about. I pumped the shotgun and looked to the flashlight carrier, who brandished a hatchet. I fired again with imperfect aim and watched the candle lighter's arm shred. It became a stump with random veins and sinew hanging out. He screamed and fell to the floor, and I stood up. I pumped the shotgun again, but the cycle didn't complete. The shell was stuck, and I was frozen. The man on the floor reached for the hatchet with his lonely left arm and flung it at me as a last-ditch effort. Unlucky for me, the hatchet was partially in my right shoulder and partially in the drywall behind me. I dropped the shotgun in pain. The hatchet was stuck, and I instantly regretted trying to pull it out. Once he was on his feet, he limped towards me and shouted, "You're the sacrifice, not me!"

He tried climbing over the bed to me, his eyes wild with murderous intent. I wanted to step away, but the hatchet was keeping me against the wall. I was going to die like a magician's assistant.

I closed my eyes, not wanting to see anymore. Then, a gunshot rang out, and I waited to feel any more pain. But when I opened my eyes, the candle lighter was motionless on the bed, with a single bullet sticking out from his forehead. If it had penetrated any further, that may have been it for me.

Gasping for air, I looked up at the bedroom doorway, and I saw my savior.

Dr. Montgomery lowered the European pistol and, without any wavering in his voice, asked, "Now, can we talk?"

CHAPTER ELEVEN

Storytime

Even though it was the right thing to do, I wasn't thrilled by the idea of calling the police again, but Dr. Montgomery insisted. Well, only after he detached me from the wall and removed the hatchet. Then, after flipping the breaker, I made the call, and we waited in the kitchen for the police to show up. He went ahead and cleaned the wound, along with sewing up the cut with a first-aid kit. It wasn't too deep, but it sure hurt like hell. He had offered a few words of reassurance as he cleaned me up, but it wasn't until after suture that he said, "I'm sorry you had to go through this."

"I suppose you warned me."

"Sure, but, how old are you?"

"Eighteen."

"Hmm. Guess you're not the only eighteen-year-old that's had to kill a man."

"I'm trying not to think about it that way," I replied. "They were savages. It was either them or me."

Dr. Montgomery nodded, replying, "I've never seen them act like this. Something must be different."

His cryptic response didn't help me much. He stayed collected and didn't comment on my logic. Maybe he agreed, maybe he didn't.

Surprised by how aloof he was, I asked, "Should I be sorry that you went through it too, or was it not your first time?"

"Police!" I heard from the front door as they pounded away.

Dr. Montgomery stepped out of the kitchen and said, "We'll talk later. Stay at the kitchen table and just tell them the truth."

I stayed put while Dr. Montgomery went to answer the door. I expected a more aggressive entrance, but voices stayed low as they walked in.

The main cop was a hefty man, with a graying mustache and gray hair under his police hat. He didn't look too old as far as his skin was concerned, but he had definitely seen a thing or two. Next was a petite blond cop, also in uniform with a similar hat to the hefty man, followed by a pale lanky man with black hair that was dressed in a suit.

"I'm Chief Rykowski, she's Officer Bailey, and the man in the suit is Detective Yamura."

"Heard you have a bit of a mess for me," Detective Yamura said with zero emotion.

"Hey, don't be weird. You said it happened in the bedroom, right?" Chief Rykowski asked. I nodded, and the chief told him to check it out. When Yamura left, the chief then asked me, "Okay, who do you want to tell your story to? Me or blondie?"

"Officer Bailey, I guess."

"Okay, you'll talk to me," the chief answered, denying my request. "Bailey, talk to the doc out in the backyard."

Officer Bailey nodded and directed Dr. Montgomery to the backyard. Yamura exclaimed something as he stepped into the bedroom, and the chief sighed.

"You'll have to excuse him. I suppose he has to have some screws loose for his job," Rykowski commented.

"It definitely is a mess in there," I replied, feeling queasy.

"Well, just take it easy and tell me the story. You don't have to be too descriptive. I know what a shotgun to the face will do to someone."

I didn't really know how much of the story he wanted, but I told the story from when I went to the church to when I left. Except, the lie I made up was claiming it was a stomach ache that made me leave the church early, and that I woke up from a nap to discover everyone outside the house. Otherwise, the rest of the story was told truthfully.

When I finished, Chief Rykowski sat back, and the chair creaked under his weight. He was messing with a toothpick and said, "A hatchet to the arm, huh? You alright?"

"Yeah, Dr. Montgomery patched me up."

"That's funny. He ain't that kind of doctor, but good on him."

"So, now what?" I asked. "Am I going to jail?"

"Shit, no. Castle doctrine, look it up. I'd say this is clear self-defense, as long as Dr. Montgomery corroborates. Whenever Yamura finishes, he'll have a team come out and clean this place up."

I wanted to feel relieved, but I wondered what Dr. Montgomery would say. He didn't know why I left the church, and he didn't know about me passing out by the front door. Deciding not to panic, I reassured myself by thinking, *How would he?*

"What about the victims? Are you going to tell their families?"

"Yeah, well, that'd be everyone else in this neighborhood besides you and the doc."

"Huh?" I asked.

Before I could get an answer, Officer Bailey brought Dr. Montgomery back inside. Montgomery gave me a look of confidence, and I felt better with his return.

"Okay, Chief, ready to discuss?"

"I don't see a need to," Chief Rykowski said as he stood up. "This family out here is queerer than a 30-dollar bill. This incident doesn't really surprise me."

"Are you saying they're all related?" I asked. "Everyone at the church? Everyone else that lives here?"

"It wasn't always that way," Dr. Montgomery said.

Right when I was about to get some answers, two women burst through the front door, screaming and crying. Nobody moved as they made their way into the kitchen.

"Thomas! Tobias! Where are they?" the two women shouted.

No one could process what to reply until Pastor Blackwood walked in behind them.

"Get the fuck out of here," I seethed.

Chief Rykowski pulled me back, and Pastor Blackwood appeared offended.

"Child, this was not done at my command."

"No one said it was?" Chief Rykowski responded.

I really only had the mental capacity for one weirdo at a time, but Yamura came out, and the women ran to him. It was odd how similar Yamura and Pastor Blackwood carried themselves, but they didn't appear to know each other.

"Where's my husband? Thomas? Is he here?"

"Oh, he's here, but he's no longer with us," Yamura said coldly.

"Good gracious!" one of the women cried out, and they both crumpled to the ground in tears.

Pastor Blackwood stepped behind them and offered a hand on one shoulder each.

"While this is a tragedy and should be treated as such, we are not wanted here," Pastor Blackwood commented. "Come back to our house. We still have plenty of chicken and tea."

Due to how fired up I was, I spat, "So first you kill my uncle's chickens, and then you try to kill me?"

"Chris, child..."

"Call me child one more time, and I'll put you in the ground."

"Easy, boy!" Chief Rykowski shouted.

Flabbergasted by my threat, Pastor Blackwood gave me one last glare before he lifted both women up and said, "Please, let us depart."

With no objections, the three of them left. Once they were out, Yamura closed the front door, so no more outbursts would happen, and the chief said, "Y'see? That's exactly what I'm talking about. Who talks like that?"

I couldn't help but laugh, but then the chief turned to me and added, "And you, I can't defend you if you're going to start talking like that to people. Okay? We're on your side. Just know that. In fact, how about we drive you into town and put you in a motel for the night?"

"I don't think that'll be necessary," Dr. Montgomery replied. "Chris, as I said before, I have an extra room. I can protect you."

"Yeah, I would like that," I replied.

"Well, you two call as soon as something happens again, and we'll be here."

"I just wish the first woman I talked to took me more seriously."

"Hmm?" Officer Bailey questioned. "You called our station?"

I nodded.

"Are you sure you called the right station?" Officer Bailey replied. "I've been in the dispatch room most of the night. Haven't heard a peep."

"I mean, I called 9-1-1? It didn't ask me to specify a station."

"Odd," Officer Bailey said, defeated. "Still, call from Dr. Montgomery's phone if you need us. Maybe your landline is busted."

Her statement didn't make any sense, but since they were all on my side, I nodded and decided to not be a nuisance. Watching the chief and Officer Bailey leave, Yamura waved them off and then went, "I hope your landline isn't busted. I need to call in my team."

While he headed towards the kitchen phone, I turned to Dr. Montgomery, and he motioned towards the front door.

"Can I grab some stuff first?" I asked.

"Sure, if you must."

I didn't really want to see the bodies again, but I went to the master bedroom. When I stepped in, I saw Thomas and Tobias. Their lifeless, mutilated bodies made me realize the gravity of what I had done. I killed them. Well, I only killed one and hurt the other really bad, but that didn't help me feel any better.

As nice as Montgomery was, my paranoia was still at maximum capacity. If I was going to his house for the night, I felt the need to arm myself. I pulled the gun drawer out, took the 1911 pistol, and grabbed a nearby satchel. Afterwards, I grabbed my pajama pants with an oversized shirt and made sure they didn't have blood all over them. As I started to walk out, I heard a soft meow.

"Mr. Pickles!"

I darted to the closet and grabbed him. He was shivering but seemed to melt in my arms. I felt worse about scaring him than I did about what happened to Thomas and Tobias.

"Oh, a cat?" Dr. Montgomery asked from the hallway.

I stepped out of the crime scene bedroom and stepped up to Dr. Montgomery.

"Yeah, I just needed some clothes and the cat. If that's okay."

"Yes, please. It'll be nice to have a pet once again. Even if it is for a night."

Leaving Yamura alone, we stepped outside in the front yard, and I saw Dr. Montgomery's Acura Legend sitting in the driveway. We climbed in, and he drove us around to the other side of the neighborhood. I tried to focus on Mr. Pickles, but something told me to look outside. Sure enough, as we passed each house, all eyes were on us. The murderers. Everyone appeared to already know what happened as they watched from their windows. A small group had even gathered at the pastor's house, which was well-lit for once. I decided to stare back while I petted Mr. Pickles like I was some James Bond villain. I wasn't happy about what happened at my uncle's house, but I was glad to still be alive.

Dr. Montgomery's was the true last house on the left. He pulled in, and I immediately noticed his house was completely different from everyone else's. The house was all brick, with two elaborate stone sections on each side of the front door. The flower bed had a few pussy willows and ornamental evergreens, along with an assortment of other flowers. The house looked a lot older than the rest but in a distinguished way. Parking in the driveway, we walked up to the front door with plenty of eyes still on us. Dr. Montgomery didn't have a care in the world as he fumbled around with his keys before finding the right one. Before he could unlock the door, it swung open on its own, and we were greeted by the young lady.

"Grandpa, did you save..."

We were standing face-to-face and I remembered her name was Lisa. Her face changed from energetic to a bit bashful, maybe because she was in cotton pajamas instead of what she had worn earlier. I felt my cheeks get hot as well, and I hated to say it was love at first sight, because... well, I guess it wasn't love at first sight. I didn't feel this way when I first saw her at the church. Damn. So, I can't and won't say that.

"He actually did pretty well by himself. Come on in, Chris."

Lisa stepped aside to let us in and then closed the door behind us. The interior was rich and cozy, with an in-ground/depressed living area to the right and a kitchen off to the front left. The old white tile floor leading to the kitchen was offset by a 70's red shag carpet in the living room. To the left was an enclosed spiral staircase that I assumed led to the bedrooms. Mr. Pickles started his own tour as he jumped to the floor and ran.

"Chris, would you like some coffee or soda? I plan to talk your ear off tonight."

"Well, black coffee for me then, I guess."

"Grandpa, can you make me that cocoa-espresso?"

She took a few steps down into the living area and plopped on one of the couches. There were two couches facing each other, with love seats on the other ends. The coffee table was massive and messy, with an incomplete game of Scrabble and a nearly completed puzzle. She gave me a look, implying that I was a loser for asking for something as simple as black coffee.

"Dr. Montgomery, I'll have what she's having."

"I thought you might say that," he called from the kitchen.

She smiled and pointed to the couch across from her.

"You can sit down."

"Great, thank you."

"Oh, you can put your bag over there."

She pointed to a faux fireplace. So far, I didn't see a reason to keep the pistol near me, so I did as she offered and placed the bag down. I still had a knife in my pocket if I had to act.

Deciding to relax, I sat across from her while she watched. I didn't want to assume she liked me, and maybe it was too soon for me to like her. But she did look adorable in her pajamas. She sat with her legs folded under her while she twisted to face me. It didn't look very comfortable, but she could make her own decisions.

"Where are you from?" she asked.

"Lawton area. Have you always lived here?"

"My grandpa has. I grew up in Rochester."

"Oklahoma?"

She laughed innocently.

"No, Rochester, New York. It's upstate."

"Oh, fancy."

"It was," she said with a sigh.

"Can anyone help me carry the mugs? I'm not much of a waiter."

Rolling her eyes playfully, she said, "I'm coming."

She moved speedily off of the couch and made her way to the kitchen. She had a lot more vigor than I did, but hopefully, the drink would help. As I leaned back and popped my back, I felt a pain in my shoulder. Oh yeah, a hatchet had been there. Maybe I shouldn't stretch.

"Here you go, Chris."

Dr. Montgomery started handing me the chocolatey drink, and I reached up with my right hand. As soon as I grabbed the handle, I saw his eyes widen.

"So, you do have The Mark."

I wanted to say "No, my name is Chris," but even Lisa's facial expression changed as they looked at me like a zoo animal.

"The Mark? No, my cat scratched me."

"And then you touched your blood during a fusion," Dr. Montgomery added.

Lisa went ahead and sat down where she was before while Dr. Montgomery caressed and inspected my hand. I awkwardly held the scalding drink up in the air, wishing I could try a sip.

"Uh, Grandpa, you're creeping him out."

"Hmm?" Dr. Montgomery turned to Lisa, and then back to me. "Oh, I'm sorry. I've just never seen The Mark in person before."

"Well, what the hell does it mean?" I asked.

"Let's not jump right into that," Dr. Montgomery advised as he sat next to his granddaughter. "But at the church, that's why you left, isn't it? The spasms during their chant?"

"I thought you said you don't want to talk about my hand?"

"No, I don't want to discuss The Mark yet."

"But you just were. The Mark moved while I had the spasms."

"Fascinating," he said.

"Grandpa, he's making a point," Lisa argued.

"Ah, okay. Let us start over then, hmm?"

"Sounds great."

Dr. Montgomery took a sip of his drink and placed it on the coffee table. I took a sip of mine and could tell it was a drink for kids. The chocolate was extremely sweet, but I wouldn't complain.

"As you know, I'm Doctor Montgomery from the University of Rochester. I was a professor of Occult Sciences for most of my adult life, but about ten years ago, I inherited this house from my late parents. Around that same time, I became Lisa's guardian. Fast forward to now, and..."

"Whoa, whoa, whoa, no fast forwarding. What the hell is Occult Sciences?"

"Well, studies of the occult."

"... Yeah, still don't know what that means."

"Witchcraft and wizardry!" Lisa exclaimed.

"There's a bit more to it than that," Dr. Montgomery said. "No matter, it was a topic I took a lot of interest in, but after taking guardianship of Lisa, I had to put it aside. I just figured you'd want some backstory from us."

"Yeah, sure, that works."

"Alright. Now, in my time as a professor, I came across a lot of strange and unusual documents and stories. But I think you are starting to prove the validity of one I came across."

Standing up, he moved to the bookshelves by the fireplace and found the book he was looking for. It was pretty small and the leather binding wasn't in the best shape, but he handed the book to me and then sat back down by Lisa.

"*The Lost Papers of Lewis and Clark?*"

"Yes. Now, that's a copy of the book as it was never properly published, but sometime during their expedition, one of the men in their group was lost, never to be seen or heard from again. However, this man had quite a different account of the adventure."

"Are you going to tell me that Sacagawea was a witch?" I asked. His answer was going to determine if I would go back to my uncle's house.

"No. But she did know of Natives who practiced magic. And based on that book, magic was used during Lewis and Clark, as well as the Glenn-Fowler expedition."

"I've never even heard of that."

"Well, let's just say they named this book after Lewis and Clark's expedition for a reason. Now, the validity of this book is questioned because it talks about both expeditions, even though they were 20 years apart from one another. Which would mean, this man somehow was there for both, or it's all horseshit."

"I'm going with the latter," I commented before taking another sip.

"I could understand why. But tell me, Chris, has everything been normal since you got here?"

Sipping down the hot drink, I paused before answering, "Yeah, no, you're right. Continue."

"Now, I have read the book a few times over. So many interesting callouts, but I won't make you read it in front of us. I would just ask that you turn to page 181 and read what Isaiah Slover noted."

Delicately, the book was handed off to me, and I set the cocoa on the table. While I thumbed through the pages, Lisa grabbed a napkin and placed it under my drink as a coaster. The book was obviously photocopied, and some of the scribblings came through better than others. Following the bottom page numbers, I found 181 and started from the top.

"'January 4th, 1822. Our expedition has come to an end. We rest in the town of Santa Fe, waiting for 'morrow. The sky is so open and vast, with plenty of mountains in the distance. Some of which we had to traverse to get here. I miss my family but refuse to tell them of some discoveries we have made. This diary is for my eyes only, so that I may bear a sane face once again. Like the other regions, the Indians of this area seem to have locked away yet another beast with some kind of magic. What started as ghost stories with Lewis & Clark have now become more and more documented the farther we travel. Chief Blackwood...'"

My head jerked up, but Dr. Montgomery kept a solemn face and nodded for me to continue.

"... 'Chief Blackwood on the Verdigris River shared many stories with us before we parted in the year past. But even as we encountered the natives of the west, and now the victorious Mexicans of this Santa Fe, what I once shrugged off as folklore is starting to ground itself in our reality. Chief Blackwood mentioned the Ruling of the Six was now at a close. I pray that to be true, for if these so-called Six are still out there in the wild, I can't be certain I have a family to return to.'"

I looked up, and they both stared at me, waiting for a reaction. I didn't have much of one to give them.

"So, Chief Blackwood equals Pastor Blackwood?"

"I don't take the pastor to be over 180 years old, but there must be some lineage there."

"Okay," I said, trying to figure out what connection I was supposed to be making.

"He mentions the Ruling of the Six. Have you ever heard of that?" Montgomery asked.

"No, but I'm sure you have," I replied.

"Right, you are. In another book, *Dark Evils of the Unknown Plain...*"

"Look," I said as he started towards the bookshelf again. "You can just tell me. I don't want to keep reading passages aloud. I hated that part of school."

Lisa smirked, but Dr. Montgomery went ahead and grabbed the book before heading back to the couch once more.

"Very well, though I am a man of evidence. Based on my findings and research, the Ruling of the Six is only mentioned in *Dark Evils of the Unknown Plain*. Never formally published..."

"Always a good sign."

"... it states that there were six creatures along the Midwest and southern border of the US. Now, these weren't random cryptids. They were specific, all given different names, and some were sketched or mocked up. The Baton Rouge Boa, the Decapitating Giant, and..."

Ignoring my request, he handed me a slightly nicer book that was a bit larger than the diary. He already opened it to the page he wanted me to check, and I took it with both hands. Immediately, I was disturbed by the sketches that flooded the right side of the book, while the left side had lots and lots of text that I refused to read aloud. Skimming over it, I saw the name Blackwood a few more times, but as creepy as they were, my eyes were drawn to the sketches. They were all pencil drawings with no color, but there were enough notes off to the sides to provide a bit more detail. The creature Dr. Montgomery was showing me had a humanoid head with no hair, along with a mouth that was bigger than Aerosmith's singer. A second drawing showed the large teeth it sported and mentioned that red eyes were the last thing you'd see before you die. Moving from the head, I noticed the arched wings that were made of skin and veins. The notes mentioned the wing skin was so thin that one could see through it if there was light. The hands were somewhere between a hand and a talon, with three long claws. The feet looked like chicken feet, and it didn't look to weigh too much. My imperial measurements idiot self didn't know how big 2.4 meters tall was, but it seemed like a lot. Finally, I reached the end of the sketches and saw the supposed name at the bottom.

"The Goldie?"

"No, the Gowl-Die."

The professor's correction made my stomach sink. I could hear one of the men's voices in my head.

"That's... that's what one of them said before they tried to stab the bed. They called me a non-believer."

Dr. Montgomery nodded in solitude as he took the book back from me. I sat in confusion, baffled at what to even say next. As many blanks as he had filled in, I still couldn't solve the crossword.

"So, I don't know if I completely follow."

"By all accounts I have gathered, the Gowl-Die was sealed away in the early 1800s by Chief Blackwood, using some kind of ancient magic. Now, Pastor Blackwood intends on waking this creature from its slumber."

"Which would be bad, right?"

"I mean, for you, me, Lisa, and the rest of the world, yes. But for any of these people, no. The Gowl-Die would become their leader for the next revolution."

"I'm still confused," I admitted. "Chief Rykowski implied that everyone in this neighborhood is related. How did they pull that off?"

"My parent's house was a standalone structure for decades. It wasn't until about five years ago, that I was approached by a contractor that wanted to build houses out this way. I actually didn't want this house when I inherited it 10 years ago, and tried to sell it. But he offered to buy my parent's land to build Ruby Falls. It was a nice enough offer to where I could keep this house, but also bulk up my retirement funds. As well as have enough for raising Lisa. It seemed like the right choice at the time, but..."

"Let me guess. The contractor's name was Blackwood."

"Hank Blackwood. The pastor's father."

"Fuck."

"He built that home for his son and Madeline first. Afterwards, he built the others quickly before passing away. Before his passing, lots of new faces moved in. None of them related to the pastor. But as time went on, homeowners would disappear or vanish or drop dead, without a trace. And once the houses foreclosed, another Blackwood family would pick it up for cheap."

"Didn't the police put two and two together on people disappearing?"

"They had no evidence of foul play. But Chief Rykowski has been waiting for them to slip up, and I think your arrival finally exposed them."

"But," I started, with my stomach sinking. "You said homeowners would disappear at random without a trace. My aunt and uncle claimed they were going on a last-minute vacation... is that—"

"No, that was genuine. They left with smiles on their faces. I was close to your aunt and uncle. I forced myself to be since they were the last sane family out here. I did wonder if they were trying to leave before anything else happened."

"Yeah, I guess that's where I'm still not clear. Where exactly is the Gowl-Die?"

In a turn of events, Dr. Montgomery hesitated to answer. Instead, he looked to Lisa, who appeared peeved that he wouldn't answer.

"Your aunt and uncle's house has the Gowl-Die under it," Lisa answered.

If I was drinking anymore of the espresso, I would have spit it out. Instead, I waited to see if one of them would say they were joking. The words never arrived.

"You're telling me the Gowl-Die lives under my aunt and uncle's house?"

"Under the shelter that Pastor Blackwood paid for, yes."

"Jesus Christ... The mailman said they were digging under their house before it was built. That's why? So that they could release it? Is that all it takes?"

"To my knowledge, no. You can't just dig it up. The spell that was done 200 years ago sealed it in the ground. I would assume the shelter is just a safe place for it to spawn once the spell is lifted, as it can't be greeted by sunlight or moonlight upon resurrection."

"You sure know a lot about this thing," I said.

"Well, it's in the last book you refused to read. Also comes with the job. The Ruling of the Six is fascinating and horrifying. It's always stuck in my mind since I read about it. Can you imagine early settlers stumbling upon these monsters? Like many trade deals with the natives, there's no way they profited as much as we did when they sealed or slayed these monsters for us. However, I never expected one of the creatures to ever come back to the present world. Creatures like these could explain the lost colony of Roanoke or even the Mayans' disappearance."

"You think some of the monsters are that old?"

"Whose to say?"

"Yeah, I'd believe anything at this point. You could put an icicle up my ass and call it a fudge pop, for all I know."

Lisa laughed, but Dr. Montgomery played it safe and stayed mature.

"I think I've covered just about everything, except for The Mark."

Wishing I could keep laughing with Lisa, I stopped and replied, "What does it mean?"

Lisa's face turned serious once more, and Dr. Montgomery explained, "The Gowl-Die only takes blood from the dead. If one somehow stays alive and interrupts the fusion, you receive The Mark."

"And I'm assuming that's a bad thing."

Dr. Montgomery leaned in towards me and, with a grave face, replied, "While I don't know how or when they can summon the Gowl-Die, I do know this: The Mark means that once it's summoned, only one of you can live."

CHAPTER TWELVE

An Unexpected Guest

If I had a nickel for every ultimatum I was given in the last 24 hours, I'd have ten cents.

I fell quiet, wanting to laugh at my thought but couldn't bring myself to. I would have been the only one laughing in the room, and that didn't seem like a sane thing to do. But ever since I interrupted the fusion and obtained The Mark, I knew something had changed. If the church incident wasn't proof enough, Dr. Montgomery's remarks were enough to seal my fate. In the end, it was going to be me or the Gowl-Die.

Lisa stared with caring eyes, while Dr. Montgomery was also at an impasse on what to say next. The man with all the answers had finally gone silent.

Eventually, the phone rang from the kitchen, and Dr. Montgomery went to retrieve it. Lisa and I were alone in the living room, and she finally broke eye contact with me to stare down at the ground. No one knew how to comfort me, but I wasn't sure I even needed it.

"Hmm, no, we sure didn't... Chris, can you come to the phone?"

Happy to have an excuse to stand up, I walked to the dark green kitchen and stepped to Dr. Montgomery.

"It's Yamura," he informed.

I took the phone and Dr. Montgomery stepped aside, watching me.

"Hey, Chris?"

"Yes?"

"Just wanted to check with you. Y'all didn't come by and do any cleaning of the crime scene, did you?"

"Uh, no. We've been at Montgomery's residence for a while now."

"Okay. I might have to get another cleaning crew out to your uncle's tomorrow, then. I think some blood went under the floorboards of their bedroom. So weird, though… nothing on the bed anymore besides their bodies. Like they're drained."

Knowing all too well what he was referring to, I said, "My aunt and uncle, they like staying state-of-the-art with water-repellent sheets and technology."

"But the living room just has an eight-track."

"Did you have any other questions?" I asked, already dismissive.

"Nope. You should be good to come back in the morning. Just don't sleep in their bedroom until we get the other cleaning crew out here. Or, stay at Montgomery's."

"Okay, thanks."

The line disconnected, and I placed the phone down. Dr. Montgomery stood behind me, and he said, "You know what that means?"

"Another fusion?" I answered.

"Precisely. And while I don't know how to summon the Gowl-Die, more blood won't hurt it."

"You sure it's not in one of your billion books?"

He smiled and patted my left shoulder.

"If it is, I'll keep looking. You, on the other hand, should rest. I'll show you to your room."

We walked out from the kitchen and back into the living area, only to see Lisa still on the couch with a book in her hands.

"Lisa, I'm taking our guest to his room. I don't expect you to stay up as late as I."

"I won't, Grandpa."

We made our way up the fat staircase and entered a long hallway.

"The first guest room is here on the left. First room on the right is Lisa's. Then the second room on the left is another guest room, then my second study is on the right. And that's my bedroom at the very end."

"So, guest room one for me?"

"I'd prefer you choose the second. We don't get around to cleaning the first one very often."

"Okay," I said, and I stepped up to the second room on the left. Dr. Montgomery was following closely behind me, so I turned to face him before heading in.

"Chris. I don't expect them to attack us here, but if they do, please take this."

Out from under his coat, he pulled an old Walther P38 pistol and handed it to me.

"Eight rounds. Aim for the chest or head," he advised.

Thinking back to the carnage I inflicted just hours ago, I reluctantly nodded and replied, "Thank you so much, for everything. I think I'd be dead if you didn't.show up."

"Lisa was worried about you when you darted from the church. And when I saw the mob, I became worried too."

He patted me again, but this time on the wrong shoulder. I grimaced, and he went, "Damn, sorry."

"It's okay. Chief wasn't lying when he said you weren't that kind of doctor."

"Hah. What a jerk. Get some sleep."

Dr. Montgomery turned and made his way back down the stairs. I went ahead and stepped into the room. The bed was made for royalty, with a million pillows of various sizes perfectly assorted on a lush red comforter. There was also a vanity and a roll-top desk, but I didn't plan to use either of them. In fact, where I was once wired because of the espresso, I was now yearning for a nice bed without anyone's blood or brains on it.

"How the hell am I going to explain any of this to my aunt and uncle?" I asked myself as I approached the bed.

Wanting to absolutely crumble, I found myself stalled by a knock at the door. Remembering I had a gun in my hand, I placed it atop the rolltop desk and went to answer the door. I expected Dr. Montgomery but opened the door to Miss Montgomery. Well, if that was her last name. She stood at the doorway, carrying my satchel and Mr. Pickles, which made her even cuter than before.

"You left your bag downstairs, along with your cat."

"I'll just take the bag," I said, but once Mr. Pickles glared, I added, "Kidding. Yes, of course, you can come in, too."

"Perfect."

Misunderstanding me, Lisa made her way to my bed and jumped on with Mr. Pickles still in her arms. He didn't seem to mind, but I said, "Oh, uh, can you be in here?"

"Yeah, my grandpa isn't overbearing. Close the door, otherwise, we can't keep an eye on your cat."

A girl... in my bed? Was Ruby Falls a different planet altogether? She was coming off as innocent, though. Not like those damn pom girls back in my hometown. Kidding.

I did as she said and closed the door. My heart was thumping, but I tried to keep it cool. She had me figured out immediately as she asked, "What? Never had a girl in your room?"

"No, actually."

"Well, don't think too much of it. Even though I've lived here ten years and have only been able to talk to my grandpa the entire time. Can you imagine?"

"No," I answered while missing my grandpa's stories. Lisa patted the bed for me to sit next to her, so I did. For whatever reason, I was still nervous. Seeing a bathroom on the other side of the bedroom, I said, "Hey, I'm not going to let you be the only one wearing jammies. I'll be right back."

I disappeared to the bathroom with the satchel and closed the door. Switching to the pajama pants and an oversized shirt, I took a deep breath and then asked, "But I'm sure your grandpa has told you a lot of cool stuff, huh?"

I stepped out of the bathroom and she seemed unimpressed with my blue plaid pants.

"Sometimes, I don't know if I even see him like a grandpa," she replied while giving Mr. Pickles all the love in the world. "He took guardianship of me, moved me out here, has been homeschooling me and training me ever since."

"Training?"

"Yeah."

She set Mr. Pickles down and started lifting her pajama shirt. More entranced than I should have been, I stared and didn't even realize she was pulling a knife on me until it was up at my throat.

"Trained to protect myself."

"Shit! Okay, you made your point."

She pulled the knife away with a smile. I wasn't sure which one would kill me faster. Then, she barely lifted her shirt once more to put the knife in its sheath.

"I don't think I'll need to protect myself from you. But you've gotten a fair warning."

"Yeah, I'd say I have."

Mr. Pickles rubbed my arm for a second but went right back to Lisa. She gladly scooped him up once more and said, "I'm sorry. I feel so odd right now. I want to trust you since I haven't had a friend in ten years, but I also just met you."

"Well, you're on my bed."

"Erm, my house, my bed. So, you're the guest. Not me."

"Sure."

She was trying to be friendly, but I wasn't in the mood. Just moments ago, I was wanting to fall asleep. Now, my heart was pounding from being so close to a girl. Or maybe it was the knife. Or the espresso.

I realized I was killing the mood, so I asked, "What does 'training' entail?"

"Self-defense, mostly. But a bit of offensive measures as well. Close-quarters, long-range, you name it."

"So, what, your grandpa made you a soldier?"

"You could say that. Or I'm just a general badass."

"I can tell."

She laughed, and I couldn't help but laugh with her.

"Do you plan to follow your grandpa's footsteps?"

"Huh? You mean, teaching? No, I don't think so. That takes a special amount of patience that I don't have. I can be taught, but I hate to teach."

"Oh, I was hoping you'd show me some moves."

"We could, but I don't want to hurt you."

Still feeling a stinging in my shoulder, I defied it and said, "Just go easy on me."

With a grin, she jumped off the bed, ready to burn off the energy from the espresso. I, on the other hand, still had sleep heavily on my mind. But it was nice to talk to someone so energetic.

"Okay, how about for every move I show you, you have to ask me a question that has nothing to do with the move?" Lisa requested.

"As long as I'm still conscious by the end of this, sure."

She said she couldn't make any promises, and then the lesson began.

"Alright. Stand still," she directed.

"Oh, would your attacker be standing still?" I mocked.

"Hey, you said you wanted to stay conscious," Lisa replied.

"Fair enough."

I stood still, trying to give her enough room. A few pillows were littered on the ground behind me, and then she stood across from me. She jumped side-to-side, hyping herself up. Before I could make another joke, she stepped left, then placed her right leg behind my legs at a slant, and jammed an open palm into my chest. I felt gravity do its job as I fell straight back and slammed onto the pillows. They tried their best to break my fall, but it still hurt. As I coughed, she asked, "Where's the question?"

"Yeah, okay, uh," I said as I stood up. "How old are you?"

"18. Graduated when I was 16. Perks of homeschooling."

Now, she reached into her pocket and took out a smaller knife. She didn't fold the blade out and reassured me our lesson wouldn't result in bloodshed.

"Here," she said, and she grabbed the P38 off of the rolltop desk. She ejected the magazine, cleared the barrel, and handed it to me. "You play the bad guy, but this time, you have a gun. Just raise it from your waist like it was in a holster."

"Why don't we try this with the gun loaded?"

"Shut up, jackass."

Of course, I wasn't serious. I didn't plan on shooting anyone else for the rest of the night. Especially not Montgomery's granddaughter.

I held the pistol lamely at my side. Lisa gave me a look to take this seriously, so I jumped in place a few times and shook my head. When I thought she was least expecting it, I raised the pistol with my right hand and tried to aim for her head. Her reflexes made quick work of me, though. Using the back of her left hand, she smacked the gun away, then held me by the wrist before bringing the knife over to cut my inner elbow, and then a slash across my neck. Using my imagination, the move did seem devastating. She broke out of formation and stepped back from me.

"The next question?" she asked.

I did want to ask about the move, but I remembered the rules. Instead, I asked, "Any brothers or sisters? Or your parents?"

"Hmm, you just reminded me. Try bringing the gun up with two hands. One to hold and fire, the other to stabilize."

She mimed the stance for me first, and after a second, I followed suit.

"That didn't answer my question," I said, acting like I was threatening her with the gun.

"You asked two questions," she corrected.

She followed the same basic movement as before, but after the initial slap to push the gun away, she slashed both of my arms before going for the neck.

"Two questions; two moves. No siblings; Parents were killed."

She stepped back, and I noticed I had hit a nerve. She wasn't expressing as much joy as before, but it was understandable with her answers.

"One more move. You better have a good question for me. When you're ready, try to kick me."

I wanted to say sorry, but she wasn't interested in my apology. She was just ready to kick my ass. Taking a breath, I thought about the last karate movie I watched and did my best impersonation. She easily caught my leg and jammed the knife under my jaw. Her face was close to mine, and she was shaking.

"Hey, this was all just for fun, right?"

I'm not much of a romantic, but something told me to kiss her as we locked eyes. Before I could even complete my thought, she broke away and turned her back to me. She sounded distraught as she said, "I don't know if my grandpa was completely honest with you."

"Huh?" I replied. "What do you mean?"

She turned to me with teary eyes and said, "Since you have The Mark, it's possible that if the Gowl-Die is killed first, you will inherit its power."

"Well, can't I just reject it?"

"I... I don't think so."

"So, what? You'll have to use these moves on me if I take its power?"

"Maybe."

"So, it's either the Gowl-Die first, or me... but either way, I'm screwed?"

Of course, he hadn't told me the truth. Why would he? It's not a great feeling to have to tell someone they're going to die no matter what they do. All because I had to touch my blood in the basement. But even though the news was for me, Lisa was crying. I put the P38 aside and stepped up to her, hoping to console her.

"I don't understand. Why are you upset?"

"Why? Because you're innocent! You're not part of this freak group that my grandpa refuses to take out. He's waiting around, thinking there will be a better time to strike, but there won't. The Blackwoods have killed so many, but there's no solid proof. Why can't we get away with the same so more people like you don't have to die?"

Her voice was shaking, but her tears were minimal. I could tell she had been through a lot, and it was all bubbling out. All over the fact that silly old me was about to have to meet his maker.

"Hey," I said, and I grabbed her shoulders. The hatchet wound stung, but I refused to let that stop me. "Y'know the way I see it? If this Gowl-Die thing can be sealed away for 200 years, why can't it just fuck off for another 200?"

Her smile through the pain made my comment worth it. She looked up at me with her lips pouted out. It seemed too soon and perfect at the same time. Without delay, I went in for a kiss, and we embraced. The kissing continued and escalated, but when we got under the covers, the kissing slowed, and she broke off.

"I... we, can't do any more than that."

"Oh, yeah, of course. I'm sorry."

"Don't be," she said with a smile.

We stared into each other's eyes, and I felt safe with her. She wasn't like anyone I had ever met. But after she turned to shut the lamp off, she scooted back towards me, and I put my arms around her. And at some point in the night, Mr. Pickles fell asleep on top of us.

Chapter Thirteen

Who Can I Trust?

Waking up Monday morning next to Lisa provided me with a feeling of comfort I hadn't felt in my entire life. She was so quiet and still, while my right arm draped over her. I didn't want to move, but I definitely needed to use the bathroom. I also hoped Dr. Montgomery wouldn't get the wrong idea if he decided to burst in.

I moved, and she stirred, still dreaming about something. The doorway to the bathroom was in my sights, just needed to break free. Slipping out as gently as I could without waking Lisa or Mr. Pickles, I stood up and snuck to the bathroom on the opposite side. Being in here so briefly the day before, I only just now noticed the two sinks, a toilet, and a tub, with a door on the other side. My curiosity was getting the best of me, but I figured not peeing my pants was the first priority.

I closed the door and relieved myself. Not that it should be a surprise to me, but The Mark was still on my hand. It wasn't moving or burning, so I'd take that as a good sign. But, I debated on how I should feel about it. On one hand... Okay, maybe that phrase is a bit too poignant. Whatever. Why did Dr. Montgomery feel the need to lie to me? I was a big boy, I think I could handle him telling me I was going to die. But he had first said it would be me OR the Gowl-Die, not that both of us had to go. Did I trust him more than Lisa? He had a teaching degree, after all.

It was impossible to flush a toilet quietly, so I just went for it. While it flushed, I turned to the sink and briskly washed my hands. The toilet wasn't even done flushing as I lazily wiped my hands and headed for the other door. It opened easily, and I found myself in the first guest room that I was told wasn't clean. Not only was it clean, but it wasn't much of a bedroom either.

"Probably something else you and my uncle could talk about."

Guns, knives, swords, katanas, nunchucks: You name it, and it was hanging from the walls. Some of the guns were more for show and definitely not feasible in modern-day warfare, but others were more recent and appeared to be dust-free. Another armament for two people that could satisfy a hundred. Two houses in Ruby Falls had enough guns for the entire neighborhood. It made me wonder what other houses owned.

"Not so cozy in this room, huh?"

I turned to face Lisa as she stepped in from the Jack-n-Jill bathroom. She didn't look like someone who had just woken up, so I wondered if she was asleep when I got up.

"Yeah, not really," I replied.

She stepped up to me and gave me a hug.

"I appreciate you being a gentleman."

"You're welcome. Thanks for not knocking me out."

"Hah," she replied as she stepped back. "There's always more time for that. But are you hungry?"

"Sure."

Going back through the adjoining bathroom, we made our way back into guest room two and I tried to go ahead and open the door for Lisa to enter the hallway. Lisa wasn't in as much of a hurry as she grabbed Mr. Pickles and offered to carry him downstairs. Once we were out in the hallway, we made our way to the stairwell and were greeted by the professor himself.

"Ah, did you both wake up at the same time?" he asked, either ignorant or ignoring the sleepover.

"Yeah, the kitty here woke us up for food," Lisa lied.

"Ah, well, I mostly have human food, but we'll figure something out."

We went downstairs, and I smelled toast. My stomach growled, and Dr. Montgomery offered, "I made myself two pieces of toast with peanut butter, honey, and banana. Lisa just likes Corn Flakes with banana or strawberry. Which one of those sounds good to you?"

I picked the luxurious toast option, and he went to work. I offered to make it myself, but he declined. The island in the middle of the kitchen housed the oven, stove, and a bar with stools. Lisa was already sitting at the bar, and I joined her. When the toast popped up, Dr. Montgomery nabbed it and started dressing it. His eyes darted over to us, and he said, "From sitting across from each other to sitting next to each other, huh? You must be special if Lisa has taken a liking to you."

"Well, I do have The Mark, after all."

"You're quite nonchalant about it," Dr. Montgomery commented. "Maybe you didn't understand what I said last night."

"No, I understood. You said it's either him or me, and I'm choosing me."

"As the victor?" Dr. Montgomery clarified. I nodded, and he smiled with twinkling eyes. "That's the spirit, Chris. I like it."

He served me a plate, and Mr. Pickles was trying to determine if he could jump all the way onto the bar. It was quite a distance, but he went for it. Lisa laughed, and Dr. Montgomery seemed a bit annoyed but refused to act.

"Let's see, what do I have for the cat to eat?"

He looked around for something while I wolfed down my toast. I was happy to eat their food because I was pretty sure my rations at my uncle's house were depleted. With what little I brought, anyway. Lisa gave me a look, implying I had pigged out without displaying any manners. I took a napkin and wiped my face, and she shook her head.

"I mean, I have tuna, but that might be a little too rich," Dr. Montgomery sighed, digging through his pantries.

"Y'know, I was thinking, might be best for me to head back."

"Good idea. We'll go back, grab his food and treats, and then come back here," Dr. Montgomery stated.

"No, I mean, I thank you for your hospitality, but I'd like to go back to my uncle's."

"What?" Lisa asked incredulously. "What are you talking about?"

"You're more than welcome to stay here, Chris. We can protect you."

"I know, but I don't want to put you all at risk."

"You're putting yourself at risk by going back over there alone. You'll be a sitting duck," Lisa argued.

Mr. Pickles cried for food, and Dr. Montgomery tried patting him instead. Lisa and Dr. Montgomery were worried about me, but I couldn't let them affect my decision. I didn't want to put them in harm's way anymore, and I didn't know if I could fully trust them after receiving the mixed answers last night. Trying to put them at ease, I replied, "Okay, if you all insist, I'll come back over after lunchtime. But I just want some time alone. And I'd rather grab some weapons from my uncle's house for whatever is coming."

"Good idea. We can come pick you up sometime after lunch, and I'll help you haul some weapons back here. I'd recommend we do bring your cat back here, as well. If they summon the Gowl-Die soon, I'm not sure your uncle's house will survive."

* * *

It was around 11am when they decided to drive me back to my uncle's house. Mr. Pickles was not pleased as he made sounds like he was starving to death. Speaking of no one liking me, Lisa was still annoyed when they dropped me off, but I couldn't change how I felt. I needed to be alone and think about everything that was at stake. Holding and kissing Lisa was nice, but did she only do that to gain my trust faster? I just couldn't be sure. Plus, it was going to be hard to think about it or talk it out with them listening to me. As bold as I had been in the church, I didn't plan on calling Lisa or her grandfather out to their faces after they watched over me.

Making sure the satchel was over my left shoulder, I stepped out of the car and reached back in for Mr. Pickles.

"I can bring him up to the house if you open my door," Lisa said while holding him.

"That's a good idea."

"Let me come in, as well. I can clear it for you," Dr. Montgomery offered.

"That'd be nice, thank you."

We all headed to the front door and saw a yellow note on it. The handwriting was terrible, but it was from Yamura, stating he'd be back sometime today with the better cleaning crew. I grabbed the doorknob and found the door to be unlocked.

"Jesus. I hope someone in the neighborhood didn't take advantage of your open house," Dr. Montgomery said, as he brandished a pistol from under his coat and cocked it.

I stepped away from the door so Dr. Montgomery could start clearing it. Looking out to the other houses, I didn't see anyone looking back at me for once. Where my uncle's house had once acted as a shrine to the Gowl-Die, it was now a tombstone for the fallen.

Lisa offered to clear half of the house with Dr. Montgomery, but he refused. Mr. Pickles didn't take no for an answer as he leapt straight into the house and made his way to his food bowl.

"Man, he was really hungry," Lisa commented.

"Yeah, he was almost a goner."

Her laugh didn't last long as she felt the need to ask me again, "Are you sure you want to stay here?"

"Lisa, it's just for a few hours."

"Are you mad that I didn't have sex with you last night?"

"What?" I replied. "No. I barely know what sex is."

Not as mad as before, her voice dropped, and she replied, "I envy you, then."

Part of me wanted to ask her to elaborate, but Dr. Montgomery approached us once more and said, "Alright, Chris, you're clear. But we will come back for you in a few hours, okay? And we won't take no for an answer."

"You got it," I replied.

We amicably parted ways, and I stepped into my uncle's house. Remembering when I stepped in Thursday night, there were some things that were the same and some things that were very different. The house smelled of cleaning products, but they weren't any that Aunt Misty would use. Most of the lights were off, but now it bothered me in a new way. There were still a few chickens out back, but they moped around. A sobering feeling washed over me as I started remembering everything that happened up to this point. If I didn't answer that call at the corner store. If I didn't punch Todd in the face. If I didn't tell off my principal. If I didn't fool around with Jasmine.

I wanted to blame one of those events, but it seemed I was the main character in all of them. When was I finally going to take responsibility for my own actions and decisions?

I felt frustrated with myself, and I was glad the Montgomerys finally left me alone. Fuming with anger, I ran to the couch and started pummeling my fists into the cushions. I needed to throw a fit like a little kid, otherwise I never knew how I was going to feel any better. Lisa told me that I was going to die, so I felt I deserved a selfish outburst.

When I was done, I looked up from the couch in tears and saw Mr. Pickles staring at me from the kitchen. Before I could say anything, he squatted and began pooping on the hardwood floor. I felt I had literally scared the shit out of him, or he was just that backed up. When he finished, he ran away disgraced and embarrassed, and I couldn't help but laugh.

"Christ, okay. I'll clean it up."

It would have been nice to have Yamura's men clean it, but oh well. I walked to the kitchen and pinched my nose after I caught a whiff. It was quite foul, so I made myself pick up the pace and get it out of the house ASAP. Grabbing way too many paper towels, I grabbed it, ran out to the garage, found a tin trash can, and threw it away. When I walked back in, Mr. Pickles ran up and rubbed my legs at the door.

"What, I'm not mad at you, buddy."

It wasn't until I looked up that I saw what may have caused him to run to me.

"Child Chris."

CHAPTER FOURTEEN

An Unwelcomed Guest or Two

S tanding before me was Pastor Blackwood and Madeline. I couldn't believe it. I wanted to assume I was hallucinating, but I wasn't. Reaching into the satchel, I hunted for the 1911 pistol, but it was gone.

Where the hell did it go?

"The front door was ajar, and we wanted to check on you," Madeline said softly.

They both stared at me with seemingly harmless motives, but I couldn't hold back.

"Gah, fuck!" I yelled as I threw the satchel off my shoulder. They stood perfectly still, and I continued, "Do you two just make a buck off of every lie you tell? I closed the front door, but I probably didn't lock it because I'm a fucking idiot, and now you two are here, probably to slice me up or kill me or something because I'm a non-believer or whatever T&T said because you all believe in some bullshit thing called the Gowl-Die and now I'm 'going-to-die' because I..."

"Chris," Pastor Blackwood started, and he pointed to the picnic basket Madeline was holding.

"If that's chicken, I'm not interested," I replied, trying to calm down.

"Nope! Turkey sandwiches," Madeline replied with a lake-sized smile.

I wanted to continue yelling at them, or even to run back and get whatever gun I could and claim they had broken in aggressively, but it seemed impossible to get away with killing a woman with a picnic basket.

Feeling out of my mind, I decided to be civil as I responded, "What do you want?"

"Just your time, really. If you'll allow it," Pastor Blackwood requested.

Mr. Pickles wasn't thrilled with the idea, but I shrugged and said, "Sure."

"That's great, Chris. Thank you so much," Pastor Blackwood said, seemingly genuine. "Madeline, you brought the lemonade packets, right? Why don't you whip some up in the kitchen while Chris and I make a spot in the backyard?"

"You got it!"

Madeline acted like nothing terrible had happened in this house to her in-laws as she jumped on the opportunity to make lemonade. Pastor Blackwood carried a blanket with one hand and had the nerve to place his other hand flat on my back to lead me out to the backyard. Weirdly enough, I was starting to see their arrival as an opportunity rather than how I had initially seen it. Which was... not great.

We stepped outside, and the sun flickered as the clouds moved around. I hadn't seen so many days of clouds with no rain before, but something was brewing to the south. As Pastor Blackwood stepped out to the yard, I turned back to the perfectly good tables and chairs on the patio and asked, "Are we really wanting to have a picnic? Like, where we sit on the ground? Because I'm okay with a regular table and chairs."

"That sounds better to me, as well," Pastor Blackwood agreed.

Soon after answering, he flailed the blanket onto a nearby metal table and let it hang off of the sides. He motioned for me to sit down, so I did without arguing. Knowing I was full of dogshit decision-making lately, some part of me hoped that maybe eating with them will open dialogue for some answers. But why would I trust the pastor over the professor?

Once we were seated, Madeline brought out the picnic basket and a large pitcher of lemonade. I could still see some of the powder at the bottom that hadn't been mixed in, but I didn't plan on critiquing her to her face. She sat down after placing the pitcher and basket at the center of the table. She delicately opened the basket and pulled out pre-wrapped sandwiches. They even had our names written on them in black marker. I thanked her for my sandwich and unwrapped it. Inside was a sliced sandwich, some carrots, and a pickle spear.

"Well, if you made my uncle's chickens as fancy as you made these, then I really missed out."

"Why thank you, honey," Madeline happily replied, completely fine with my accusation.

Pastor Blackwood wasn't crazy about my comment, but he finally said, "You're right, Chris. See, I called you Chris. I know I slipped up earlier and called you Child Chris, but I won't say it anymore going forward. How's that?"

"Thank God."

"And Chris," Madeline started. "I wasn't there the night it happened, but I'm so sorry about Thomas and Tobias. I'm sure you feel some grief, too."

"I mean, they wanted to kill me. Said that they hoped the Gowl-Die would accept the blood of a non-believer."

"You're able to recall all of that?"

"Yeah, well, professor of catapult studies on the other side of the neighborhood helped me fill in some of the blanks."

"Professor of the...? Oh, I understand. Clever," Pastor Blackwood said without laughing or smiling.

I was hoping they would take over the conversation, as I was having to take tiny bites between each comment. I felt strange, trying to joke around with my assumed enemy.

"I apologize as well, Chris. I can promise to whatever deity you see fit that they acted alone."

"You would swear to the Gowl-Die, then?" I asked.

His hesitation answered me right away, but he went ahead and clarified, "Did I command them to go kill you? No. But did they misunderstand me when I said you were the key to bringing our leader back from its eternal damnation? Yes, they very much did.”

“Huh,” I said, taking a bite of some baby carrots.

“Chris, I know my... or our neighbor told you about the Gowl-Die, but do you even understand what it is?”

“Yeah, I know it’s the ugliest motherfucker this side of the Mississippi.”

Pinching a nerve with Pastor Blackwood, he scowled and replied, “I will not tolerate your insults of my god.”

“I’m sorry. Come to think of it, there are some uglier people out here.”

“Thank you,” Pastor Blackwood replied sincerely. “Our cause, it’s not one to be taken lightly. We have an opportunity to bring back one of the most powerful creatures the world has ever seen.”

“But, isn’t that going to piss off your great-great-great-great-grandfather who placed it under the spell to begin with?”

“He was cornered by the settlers. If he had a choice, he wouldn’t have sealed the Gowl-Die away. I think he should have stood his ground, but maybe I would have done the same if I was there.”

“So, all you care about is the Gowl-Die. Not the other monsters from the Ruling of the Six?”

“Very good, Chris. Wow, Dr. Montgomery truly must have filled you in last night.”

“Yeah, with knowledge and some really sweet cocoa/coffee drink.”

“Good on him. Although, I’m sure he isn’t a fan of mine. No matter. I would only try to befriend him if he had a book on how to summon the Gowl-Die.”

“Wait,” I said, hoping to finally get some good news. “You mean, you don’t know how to summon it?”

“Chief Blackwood used an old spell book to seal it away. That book was lost in a housefire way before I was even born. Otherwise, I’d have the spell to recite to bring it back with ease.”

"Oh, bummer," I said, trying to contain my happiness.

"But, we do know of two other ways to summon it. One is to sacrifice a virgin, aged 16 to 19, and the other way is not one I'd want to commit to."

"Are you saying you know I'm a virgin?"

"Yes. I can sense it."

"Uh, okay. Is it how I dress, or..."

"No. It's an ability I was given by my grandmother. I can sense the purity of an individual. It was really intended as an ability to find the perfect love, but I'm able to sense it from others as well, even after finding my love."

Madeline and Pastor Blackwood held hands and shared a loving look. There were so many insults I wanted to throw at Pastor Blackwood. It also made me wonder why he called me Child, but I wanted to leave that alone.

"Why summon it, though?" I asked.

"The Gowl-Die?"

Pastor Blackwood's clarification made my eyes roll back so hard that I may have torn an optic nerve. Trying to keep it together, I replied, "Yes, the Gowl-Die."

He placed his sandwich down and softly wiped his face before responding, "Well, simply put, I'm not happy with the world we live in. I want us to live in a simpler time, with simpler rules. I don't care about capitalism. I don't care about the free market. You must have heard or seen what happened in the stock market back in '87. Why must we rely on a system like that? Why must we be at war yet again with another country? Why be so complacent when we can have something better?"

"And something better to you is a ravenous monster?"

"Not a monster, Chris. A leader. A guardian. With speed and strength unmatched by any mortal. And by releasing the Gowl-Die, we will be in its favor. If we don't summon it, the spell itself may wear off, and it will see no one as an ally. We are just trying to be ahead of the curve."

"Haven't you had other virgins in this town?" I asked.

"We thought Lisa was one, but..."

Pastor Blackwood stopped himself. It was weird seeing him show any kind of empathy to anyone other than his family and the Gowl-Die. But then, I thought about how suddenly our kissing stopped. Poor Lisa.

"So, you want to kill me, drain my blood, and then have a big party for the Gowl-Die?"

"Tonight, yes. A new moon on Monday."

"Tonight!" I shouted. "And your way of swooning me was to feed me lunch? Madeline, if someone has told you your sandwiches were to die for, I don't think they meant it literally."

Pastor Blackwood leaned into me and coldly explained, "I felt the need to come clean to you. Be honest with you. You can help our cause by summoning the Gowl-Die, and by accepting your blood, the Gowl-Die will look favorably upon your family. You don't want them to suffer once it's summoned, right? You can do the right thing."

They both stared at me, wanting an immediate answer. What the hell did they expect me to say?

Yeah sure, I'd love to die for the Gowl-Die that I just learned about less than 24 hours ago. Sounds swell.

But I stared back and decided to be honest with the one person I shouldn't have been honest with.

"Well, I hate to break it to you, but I don't think I can be the sacrifice."

"And why is that?" Pastor Blackwood asked, annoyed.

Without hesitating, I raised my hand and lowered the sleeve on my oversized shirt to reveal The Mark. Pastor Blackwood flew backward so fast that he lost his balance and fell out of the chair, kicking the table up. Lemonade flew in the air as the pitcher shattered on the ground. It was quite the opposite of how Dr. Montgomery reacted, but I figured it was due to me ruining their perfect plan.

"No," Pastor Blackwood said as he collected himself. "No, no, no, no... I'm going to be sick."

Madeline gasped as Pastor Blackwood dashed into the house, hand covering his mouth. I could see him through the windows as he made his way to the bathroom. Once he was out of view, Madeline looked at me, and her face shifted.

"You need to get out of here," she said to me in a completely different voice.

"Why? What's going on?"

"You have The Mark!"

"Yeah, I've been told. But what does it mean?"

Madeline was shaking, crying, and panting.

"Not only are we unable to use your blood for the sacrifice, but you have to be killed once the Gowl-Die is summoned. There's no other way around it."

"I, I, I don't have a vehicle or a way to get out of here," I stammered.

"I can help you. I'm over this shit. I've played along for too long. I turned a blind eye to the original neighbors disappearing. I was hoping the police would arrest him after Thomas and Tobias, but that was wishful thinking. At this point, we just need to run. I can drive you out of town. Now, while he's sick!"

Already feeling the urgency in her voice, she grabbed my arm and started dragging me to the back door so we could go inside. Once inside, I started to pull back and ask to grab supplies, but she told me no. I pleaded, probably making way too much noise as we crossed the living room. And once we were at the front door, she stopped.

"Fine, fine, get your stupid—"

She had turned back to face the living room, and a gunshot rang out. I jolted. The force of the bullet flattened her to the front door, and she slid down, lifeless. Blood spilled from her right eye like a red river, and her hand muscles slowly released my arm. Pastor Blackwood stood in the living room, a smoking gun in his hand.

"Never thought my own wife would turn against me. There must be something about you, Chris."

He stepped towards me, and I faintly felt a knife in my pocket. He kept the gun on me as his other hand reached into his coat pocket. When whatever he was grabbing got stuck, I yanked the knife out, flipped it, and charged. I stabbed into his upper chest near his shoulder, but the knife didn't go very far. Barely reacting, he looked down at me and said, "I have something for you, too."

Surprised he didn't just shoot me, he revealed a syringe and plunged it into my bicep. I pushed him away, but everything started going hazy. My strength was leaving my body. And before I went under, I heard him shout, "The TIME is NOW!"

CHAPTER FIFTEEN

Kingfisher Police Department

"Oh, it's a Monday, alright."

Chief Rykowski sat at his desk, trying to wrap up a phone call. His pasta lunch had already been microwaved three different times, but he kept getting one more call as soon as he'd stop to eat. This latest call was a doozy. The woman on the other end of the phone had a son who was prone to being truant, and yet again, he was missing. The Chief was hoping summer would start up soon, so he wouldn't have to hear from her anymore. But the kid was getting older, so he feared that the next call about him would be something a lot more serious.

"Yes, Mrs. Barnett... Oh, you're going by your maiden name now? My apologies, Ms. French... You told me last time?... Ma'am, I talk to a lot of people inside and outside of the station, I didn't mean anything by it... Yes, Mr. Barnett was a piece of work, I'll agree to that..."

Officer Bailey poked her head in but then laughed when she heard who he was talking to. Chief Rykowski waved her away, and she took a sip of coffee from the stained Styrofoam cup. It was otherwise quiet at the station, and besides Officer Bailey and Officer Gilford, the only other person in the office at the moment was Detective Yamura.

Yamura was one knee-deep in his computer and another knee-deep in a book from the library. He always ate lunch before anyone else since he was usually up by 5am. He was only scheduled to work 8am to 6pm, but being the only detective, he stayed on call. He never slept much. Had always been single. He and Officer Bailey tried to date early on in his hiring, but it never worked out. Yamura was closest to the local bartender, but he didn't even drink alcohol. He was just naturally weird. Chief Rykowski didn't love having him employed, but he knew of his family's background. All war veterans, with most of them dying in combat. Yamura grew up alone, relying on his mother all his life until he got an academic scholarship. If it wasn't for that scholarship, Yamura might have become the next prolific serial killer, just to occupy his brain.

But now that Ruby Falls had an actual crime scene instead of random unsolved disappearances, he decided to click through the files that he had written up at the time. Thomas and Tobias were residents of Ruby Falls during every single disappearance. Were they the ones orchestrating the kidnappings? But why did they slip up so badly this time? They were deceived by a kid from out of town? It didn't make sense to him. In a way, he was glad Chris killed the two men, but it made all the other cases cold with frostbite. The sudden ending to the mystery left Yamura wanting more.

How did Thomas and Tobias dispose of the bodies? The cadaver dogs sniffed all around the neighborhood after the first few disappearances without a single hit. In fact, Chief Rykowski got tired of paying the bill to bring the dogs in, that they stopped sniffing after the fifth occurrence.

"Is there even a mystery to be solved anymore?" Yamura muttered to himself.

"What was that?" Officer Bailey asked.

"Nothing. I think I'm losing my mind."

"Oh, sweetheart, I think that happened to you a long time ago."

"Get lost."

Officer Bailey could tell her colleague was upset, so she eased up and sat down on his desk.

"What's the problem? Pissed that a kid killed your two suspects?"

"I didn't even suspect them. I suspected the pastor or the entire neighborhood in general. Especially when the family of five went missing a few years ago. How on earth does someone pull that off?"

"I don't know. That place gives me the creeps. I feel bad that you have to go back."

"Well, I'm practically doing them a favor in sending that cleaning crew out."

"Coroner already took the bodies?"

"Yeah, and he was just as confused as me."

"Oh," Officer Bailey remembered. "What was it you told me? The blood disappeared?"

"Most of it, yes. Must have slipped under the floorboards."

"Gross," Officer Bailey replied. "Count me out. When are you going back?"

"I'm still waiting to hear from the team. Another one from OKC."

"Gah damn, you're always racking up the bills around here. That's why we can't afford any better coffee."

"I'm just trying to do my job."

Officer Bailey patted Yamura's shoulder and replied, "You're doing the best you can. We all see it."

Without any subtlety, Chief Rykowski flung his door open and said, "Perfect. You two, in my office, now."

His request was stern, and it puzzled the two cops. If HR was wanting to act on their past escapades, they were a few years too late. The two of them complied and made their way to his office. The Chief didn't like standing too long, so he plopped down in his chair and pressed his phone.

"You're on speaker phone, now," Rykowski said.

"Hello, this is—"

"Our son—"

"Beaten—"

"I'm gonna kill him—"

Officer Bailey and Detective Yamura gave each other a confused look at the overlapping voices. They were hectic and flustered. Chief Rykowski sighed and said, "Hey, hey, one at a time."

The other side of the phone fell silent after some grumbling, and then a voice replied, "This is Sheriff Myers speaking out of Lawton. I hear you know where Christopher James Walker is located."

"He's a piece of shit, I'll tell you that!" another voice yelled at the other end.

"Mr. Pickley, please."

"I, uh," Yamura started. "This is Detective Yamura speaking. Yes, I know someone going by the name of Chris who's been staying at his aunt and uncle's house."

"Right, that's who we're looking for," Myers replied. "Last week, on Thursday, Chris had sexual relations with a classmate, told his principal off, and assaulted this man's son."

"Damn, Chris is kinda cool," Yamura said.

Chief Rykowski shook his head with clenched teeth, and they were glad no one heard his comment.

"Chris is dangerous," Mr. Pickley yelled. "My son's nose is destroyed, and he's going to have to wear veneers now. He's 18 years old, not 80. His parents don't even care. I fired his dad the second I heard about it, that son of a bitch."

"Are Chris' parents there?" Yamura asked.

"They don't need to be!" Mr. Pickley shouted.

"No, it's better to keep the two sets of parents separated if you can't tell," Myers commented.

"Sure," Chief Rykowski replied.

"But Chris' parents did comply as soon as they knew where their son was. Look, I'm not sure how you want to handle this, but the parents want to press charges."

"I don't want to press charges," Mr. Pickley fumed. "I want to take him out back and do a number on him, just like he did to my son!"

"A little southern justice, we could do that," Chief Rykowski agreed.

"We're midwestern?" Yamura corrected quietly.

"Either way, it'd be best if someone could round up Chris and maybe meet us halfway, so we can drive him back into Comanche County."

"I don't want to wait that long," Mr. Pickley said. "I'm ready to hop in my truck and head on up there as soon as you give me an address."

"It's kinda hard to find, but it's a neighborhood called Ruby Falls."

"Chief, wait!" Yamura exclaimed.

"Chief, you better keep your people in line," Mr. Pickley shouted.

"Screw you," Yamura replied.

"Hey!" Chief Rykowski started.

Mr. Pickley interrupted with, "Screw me? Screw you, ya fuggin—"

First, Chief Rykowski pressed the mute button, then repeatedly pressed the volume down button to temporarily silence Mr. Pickley's voice.

"Yamura, what's gotten into you?"

"Why are you okay with this?" Yamura replied. "Do you hear this man? I can only imagine what his son is like. Must be the school bully down there."

"I don't care. The law is the law. If he assaulted Mr. Pickley's son, we need to apprehend him."

"I get that, but letting this man come out here to beat Chris to death?"

"Oh, he's not going to beat him to death. We'll keep an eye on it. Honestly, it will save us a lot of paperwork in booking him."

"Lord almighty."

Seeming to be at a loss for words, Yamura stood down, and Chief Rykowski glared. Then, the chief started turning the volume back up, and they heard Mr. Pickley still ranting and raving about wanting to beat Chris up and then Yamura if he ever talked to him like that again, and so on. Once it was unmuted, Rykowski replied, "Yeah, my detective apologized. Okay, can we get on to what to do next?"

"I can pick him up," Yamura offered.

"Aw, that's gonna take too long," Mr. Pickley complained.

"Not if I meet you halfway?"

"Oh, right. Yeah, well, hurry up. You better radio in as soon as you get him, otherwise I'm heading all the way there. If you get him, we'll meet in Chickasha. There's a nice pancake house there."

"Sure thing," Yamura played along.

"Myers here. I appreciate your offering to apprehend him. Hope to hear back soon."

"Over and out," Chief Rykowski replied, and the call came to a close. Yamura started to leave, but the chief stopped him. "Hey, I can trust you to get him, right?"

"Yes, but time is a factor. I don't want that asshole driving all the way out here," Yamura said.

"Let me come with you," Officer Bailey offered.

"No, it's okay. I did try calling the house about an hour ago, and no one answered. Oh, that's right, he went to Dr. Montgomery's house."

"Well, go on, get him," Chief Rykowski encouraged.

CHAPTER SIXTEEN

The Troublemaker Finds More Trouble

Ever since I had arrived in this damned neighborhood, I wasn't good at waking up smoothly. It seemed that every instance of me trying to sleep was inhibited by something outside of my control. Whether that be a cat, or a monster, or two guys wanting to fillet me.

This time, I was stuck in a groggy state due to whatever the pastor had jabbed into me. But I was able to move, and a familiar voice helped wake me up.

"Chris!"

My eyes widened, and I could remember it wasn't the first time Lisa had tried to call out my name or shake me awake. But all those memories were foggy and distant. Whatever the serum was, I might have to ask for some before leaving this place.

Lisa knelt beside me, and when I gave her minimal signs of life, she torpedoed in to hug me. I was able to hug her back, but I felt like a deadweight as I still struggled to get up. Looking around, I realized we were in an unfamiliar space. A small room with a single dangling light, with metal walls around us.

"Where are we?" I asked.

"We're locked in some kind of panic room, next to your uncle's basement."

"How did you end up in here?"

"I should ask you the same."

"Hmm, well..."

"My grandpa and I warned you, Chris! We told you not to go back over here."

Starting to recollect what occurred before being locked in the room with Lisa, I argued, "Hey, well, I may have not been apprehended by the damn pastor if you didn't take my pistol from the satchel!"

"Take the pistol from... what?"

"Yeah, now you want to play dumb."

"Chris, I promise you. I didn't know there was a pistol in your satchel. Why would I take that when my grandpa gave you the P38?"

She seemed to be telling the truth, but I didn't know who to believe anymore. I didn't know if now was the time to debate and argue, so I let it simmer down before I asked, "Come to think of it, where is Dr. Montgomery?"

"I... I don't know," Lisa replied, worried. "It was nearing the time to go back and get you. I went looking for him in the house, but I couldn't find him. So, I tried coming to your house on my own on foot, but the entire neighborhood was out and about, and they caught me at gunpoint. Then, they dragged me down here and threw me in with you. For the last hour or so, I've been watching you sleep."

"Interesting," I replied. "Well, Pastor Blackwood and Madeline snuck in soon after you two left. They tried bribing me with turkey sandwiches and a nice picnic before they discovered I had The Mark. That's when Madeline went turncoat and tried to help me escape, but Blackwood killed her and gave me a big dose of sleepy juice."

"He killed Madeline?"

"Didn't even give her a chance."

"Dammit."

Lisa paced around the room and I stood around, trying to wake up completely. Remembering I had my uncle's watch on, I checked the time. It was about 2pm, so that sleepy juice really did it to me.

"Well, how do we get out of here?" I asked.

"I don't know."

"You're the one with all the training," I sneered. "Here, let me try something."

Not even wanting to ask, she watched as I approached the only available door in the room and tried to open it. The door rattled back and forth but wouldn't open.

"You don't think I tried that?" Lisa scolded.

"Eh, worth a shot."

I went ahead and slid down to the ground so I could sit. I wasn't at full strength and thought about a nice glass of water. Lisa looked distraught as well but appeared to have some plans floating in her head.

"Okay, let's discuss what we should do the next time they open the door," Lisa suggested.

"I'm all ears."

"Only one man has come in the last few times, but I didn't want to escape without you."

"How kind."

Lisa appeared fed up with me as she said, "Chris, if you don't trust me, then we don't have to talk about this. I can work alone and leave you here to die. I am trying to help you. Please, believe me."

Staring each other down with bated breath, I decided in that moment that it was better to trust one person than no one at all.

"Okay, alright, I'm sorry," I eventually replied. "I want to get out of here, too. Especially since Madeline said that I'll have to die once the Gowl-Die is summoned."

"So, they do know how to summon it?"

"Supposedly. And they want to do it tonight."

Lisa's eyes widened. I guess I should have mentioned that sooner, but she calmly replied, "In that case, let's make a plan."

Escape 101: Look for air vents. I knew the main part of my uncle's basement had some, but this room didn't. At the very top, there were tiny air holes that must have fed into a different ventilation system, but we couldn't fit into those. Next, I lifted Lisa onto my shoulders to see if there was a weak spot in the walls. Before lifting her up, she took a small ring off her finger and said, "Here, take this for me. Wear it on your pinky or something."

The ring was a gold band with a yellow stone in the middle. Didn't seem like anything too fancy, but I understood why she wanted to take it off. She would knock, but they wouldn't budge. Then, she checked the solid concrete floor to see if there were any cracks or hidden spots. Unfortunately, the room was sealed tight with no escape besides the front door. A panic room that induced panic instead of protecting from it.

"Okay," Lisa said, still holding onto hope. She signaled for me to be quiet as she whispered, "That means, we have to wait until someone comes to open the door for us, and then we'll take them out."

"Aren't they armed?" I asked.

"Yeah. The people outside have guns, but around the basement, they have electric cattle prods."

"Nice. Think you can use your moves to rip one of those away?"

"It'll be tricky, but maybe."

"Or, maybe your grandpa is figuring out a way to save us."

Lisa nodded and said, "Y'know, this isn't the first time I've been stuck in a situation like this."

"Oh, you've been in some other secret basement before?"

"When I officially graduated high school, Grandpa and I hunted down the Baton Rouge Boa."

"Two years ago?" I asked, and she nodded. "So, you're saying the Six still exist?"

"More or less," Lisa clarified. "The boa wasn't much of a challenge. It didn't have a fanbase like the Gowl-Die."

"So, your grandpa trained you to hunt the Six?"

Still fumbling with the walls, she stopped to look at me and said, "I was using the term 'soldier' loosely before. My grandpa said I'm a Tracker."

"How many more do you all need to track?" I asked.

"If we can kill this Gowl-Die, three. If we escape and the world doesn't end…"

I was new to all this, but it didn't seem like the best idea to leave the Gowl-Die alive. It seemed irresponsible, to say the least.

"I think we have to kill it," I responded. "If we can."

"Hopefully, fire and bullets will do the trick," Lisa sort of joked. "Or, if we can escape and take the neighborhood back, maybe we can stop the summoning."

"Yeah, about that…"

"God, what else have you forgotten to tell me?"

"Pastor Blackwood and Madeline told me that they're summoning the Gowl-Die so they can be seen as allies. They claimed that if they didn't summon it now, it might break free from the spell and summon itself."

"A spell that expires?" Lisa asked. "I mean, that's not completely out of the question. I've read about spells that needed to be maintained by a certain bloodline. But I also figure that if they summon the Gowl-Die tonight, it won't be picking favorites."

Now wishing I had the book to read so I could kill time, I sighed and checked my pockets.

"Guess we'll either wait for someone to come in here or for someone to save us," I said.

* * *

In an unmarked vehicle, Yamura pulled up next to the sign for Ruby Falls. He assumed this would go smoothly, as long as Chris didn't fight back. But if he hadn't put his coffee down in time, he wouldn't have noticed the armed presence outside of Chris' uncle's house. Luckily, no one was guarding the neighborhood entrance, so he didn't appear to alert anyone right away. Pulling the car off to the side, he parked out of the view of the residents and killed the engine. It was getting dark from the storm clouds, but Yamura felt he could handle a little rain. Debating between calling for backup or going in alone, he decided to radio back to the station.

"Chief, I don't think I can get Chris. Something is going on."

Silence, then an abrasive crackle of static before Chief Rykowski replied, "What? What do you mean?"

"The neighborhood, they're all armed and outside Chris'. Might be another mob."

"You're breaking up. You're saying you can't get to Chris? Mr. Pickley is going to flip his shit when he hears this."

Refusing to meet the man, Yamura exhaled and replied, "I'm going to try and get Chris. Stall Mr. Pickley, please. Over and out."

There was so much interference after his last communication that he felt the need to turn the radio off. Under his suit jacket in an underarm holster, he carried a Beretta 92FS. The pistol was practically stuck as he tried to take it out, and he couldn't recall the last time he shot or cleaned it. He liked the quiet nature of Kingfisher, but now he had to play the hero.

When Yamura opened his car door, he heard some of the neighbors fast approaching. Cursing to himself, he decided to book it for the tree line and sneak behind everyone's backyard until he could guess which one held Chris. He watched from the trees as the mob rounded the entryway and found his car. They all carried military-style rifles with body armor vests. The vests were kitted out with other accessories, like miscellaneous grenades and extra ammo. Yamura had about 34 bullets total on his person, making him feel outmatched. The group of adults surrounded his car, then started bashing it with the butts of their rifles.

"So long, car. Guess I'll use their vandalism to my advantage," Yamura murmured to himself.

He knew it was the fourth house on the left as he ran through the trees. He was back far enough that no one would see him, but the high grass and jumping bugs made him wonder what he'd find on himself later. No doubt there were ticks out here, but he tried to ignore that. Passing the first few houses, he remembered that Robert's was the only one with a low fence to face the woods. And sure enough, after only a bit more jogging, he found the house.

Taking a moment to survey it, he saw all the lights were on, but no one appeared to be in the living room or kitchen. With a quick prayer, he jumped the fence and made his way up to the house, a gun close to his chest. It seemed all the security detail was in front of the house, with no one in the back.

In the distance, he heard his car alarm, and he wondered if they were still beating it up. If so, he might have to steal a car just to get out of here. But would he really take Chris straight to the station so some punk's dad could beat him up? Taking him from one hellish situation to another seemed wrong. Instead, he hoped to help Chris escape and maybe throw him on the next train out of town.

Still not seeing any movement inside, Yamura reached for the backdoor handle and gently turned the knob. The knob turned easily, and he was now inside the house. Now leading the way with his gun, he walked towards the bedrooms but heard some metal thudding underneath him. He still didn't hear anyone above ground, but then he realized what the sound was.

Everyone knew about the basement. The cadaver dogs thought they caught a whiff down there, but Yamura was relieved when they didn't find anything. He liked Robert and Misty and was happy to know they weren't behind the kidnappings, or assisting with them. As far as he knew, anyway. But now, with the noise down below, he wondered if Chris was hiding or trapped.

Turning around to the garage, he poked his head out to check before entering. No one was in the garage, either, but the door was halfway open with a few adults roaming about. Not that the kids should be a part of it, but he wondered where they were or how they were being entertained. Yamura figured, in the long run, it was better for them to not be a part of whatever was going on.

Yamura quickly and quietly darted to the basement entrance and made his way down the steps. When he reached the bottom, he made sure to peek in before entering, and that's when he finally saw someone on guard duty.

All the way at the other end of the basement was a man sleeping on one of the couches. Yamura figured he could sneak up on him or even avoid him entirely. He didn't see Chris but figured he was the one making all the noise at the other end of the room.

Yamura went ahead and closed the sliding door behind him, just in case things got noisy. Bolting across the room, he could hear not one but two voices behind the couch area. Not sure who the second voice was, but he knew the first was Chris'.

Yamura knew about the panic room, as well. The door was off to the side and at an angle, so it was easy to miss. Looking down, he saw the lock and chain around the door.

"Ah, are you here to take over guard duty?"

The man on the couch was clueless as he stood up, only seeing Yamura from behind. Without fully thinking it through, Yamura turned to face the man with his gun up. He didn't even have time to say freeze as the man lifted a revolver. Yamura shot first, and the man stumbled backwards, crashing into the table.

* * *

We heard a gunshot outside of the panic room and stopped messing with the walls.

"Grandpa?" Lisa cried.

"I hope it's him," I said optimistically.

Whoever it was started fumbling around with the door, and we heard chains. Soon after, another gunshot rang out, and the door swung open. It was Detective Yamura, looking as ghost-faced as ever.

"Detective?" Lisa said, confused.

"You, too? C'mon, we gotta get out of here," Detective Yamura encouraged.

"Sounds good to me," I said.

Yamura waved for us to move out, and we left the panic room. I looked to the left and saw the man who received the first gunshot. Blood was spilling out of his gut, and he writhed in pain, not even interested in stopping us. Surely, someone above had heard the shot go off, so I worried about what awaited us.

"I had to park on the outside of the neighborhood, and they started ripping into my car," Yamura said.

"Well, unless something changed, we can try getting to my grandpa's car. His was still out front."

Yamura got to the door and said, "It's a bit far, but it'll have to work."

But when he tried to pull the door to the stairwell open, it wouldn't budge. First, he pulled at it alone, then Lisa and I tried to assist. No matter what, none of us could get it to move.

"Well, at least you got us out of the panic room," I commented.

It was as soon as we backed away from the door that it slid open. Yamura lifted his pistol but lowered it as soon as he saw who it was.

"Dr. Montgomery!" Yamura exclaimed. "Listen, can we use your car? We have to get out of here!"

Yamura, Lisa, and I were all excited about his presence. But as soon as Dr. Montgomery didn't reciprocate the feeling, I knew something was wrong. I didn't act fast enough, though. Dr. Montgomery lifted a suppressed pistol and fired three shots into Yamura's chest. Blood and bits of the shirt flew out from him, and he fell backwards, dropping his pistol and grabbing at his wounds. I wanted to go for the pistol, but Dr. Montgomery then aimed the gun at me.

"Grandpa, he was on our side!" Lisa shouted.

"Which side is that?" Dr. Montgomery replied.

And before either of us could inquire further, Pastor Blackwood stepped up behind Dr. Montgomery and patted his back.

"Excellent shots, brother."

CHAPTER SEVENTEEN

Summoning the Gowl-Die

"The TIME is NEARING."

I was getting tired of being drugged with the mystery serum. Again, I couldn't get my eyes opened fast enough to see what the hell was going on. Thinking back, I knew Yamura was killed at the hand of Dr. Montgomery, and then Pastor Blackwood called him "brother"?

"Chris, wake up, dammit!"

Lisa's searing voice once again was the driving force to wake me up. I shook my head and tried to rub my eyes, but my hands were tied down. When my vision came into focus, I wished I was asleep again.

Lisa and I had the couch area to our backs. We both had our hands tied to some cheap metal lawn chairs, and we were sitting next to one another. We were still in the basement, but the lighting was different. The fluorescents were turned off, and the candles were plentiful. To my right, I saw the shelves had been ransacked, and there was now a hastily painted circle on the ground between us and the exit. The circle was divided into sixths, and each sixth had a symbol. I could put it all together and figure out what it was symbolic of.

Up ahead were Pastor Blackwood and Dr. Montgomery, staring at their drawing and discussing their plans. I couldn't hear a word of it, but they didn't seem to care that I was awake.

"They really love pumping that stuff into me," I said.

"I got a dose of it this time, too. I can see why you wouldn't wake up."

Lisa wasn't fussing with the knots, so I didn't either.

"So, this is it?" I asked.

"Oh, it's only the beginning," Pastor Blackwood answered.

The two men made their way towards us, and I shook my head.

"Brothers, huh?" I started.

"Well, half-brothers. Same mom, different dads."

"Guess your mom loved the crazies, then."

Dr. Montgomery didn't take lightly to my comment, so he went ahead and punched me in the gut. All the air went out of my system, and I struggled to gain it back.

"Grandpa!" Lisa cried. "You can't seriously be with them? I should have known."

"Oh, Lisa, I didn't want you to know. Especially after we couldn't use you as the sacrifice."

"Stop," she said with her head down.

"What? Don't want the boyfriend knowing you're damaged goods?"

"You're sick," I spat. "Both of you."

"No, we're going to be the future. But I figured you all should watch the summoning of the Gowl-Die. Especially since once it's over, we'll have to kill Chris. Or do we let the Gowl-Die kill Chris?" Pastor Blackwood asked.

Dr. Montgomery retorted, "The Gowl-Die won't achieve full strength until it's killed a few people. And killing someone with The Mark will help it gain full power faster."

"Sounds like you did have another book on this thing," I interrupted.

"This 'thing' is about to be the greatest leader to walk the earth," Pastor Blackwood argued. "If only you didn't interrupt the fusion, or if I could have made you join us. Such a shame. The Gowl-Die would have probably enjoyed a jester."

"Y'know, I think I'm done with all your talking," I said. "Just summon the stupid thing and get it over with. What are we waiting for?"

"Oh, your enthusiasm delights me!" Pastor Blackwood said with glee. "We're waiting on the other members of our family to complete their own rituals."

"Right, right, how could I forget," I said.

"Should be any second now."

As much as the pastor had lied about this, that, and the other, he wasn't lying about the rituals. Before long, where there were once only four people in the basement, there were now almost twenty. The women of the neighborhood shuffled in, and it didn't seem that crowded. No one dared to step over the summoning circle as they made an outer circle. Each woman that entered held a vase of some kind, and I noticed some of them were crying or seemed distraught.

"The ultimate sacrifice was difficult, I'm sure. But we should be happy, for this is a joyous occasion."

The ultimate sacrifice... the men were upstairs while the women were in the basement, but no children. As one couple passed behind me, I heard sloshing in the vase. I figured it out, but Lisa cried out, "The ultimate sacrifice was to kill all the kids!"

"According to Dr. Montgomery, the blood of a child or many children should bring us the Gowl-Die," Pastor Blackwood explained.

"I can't believe this," Lisa said in distraught. "Why did you teach me to be a Tracker if we're not going to kill every monster for good?"

"The Gowl-Die was always my goal," Dr. Montgomery professed. "The boa was a way to legitimize these stories. Now, with the Gowl-Die on our side, we can defeat whatever other monster we want to. But in the end, one must be victorious."

"Look, I willingly killed my wife, but you don't have to kill your granddaughter," Pastor Blackwood offered. "There's no need. She will be protected. Maybe she'll come around."

"I fear she's too hung up on this boy. We'll kill him first, once the Gowl-Die is summoned. Then we'll see what happens."

With everyone in place, the chattering came to a close, and Pastor Blackwood raised his arms.

"Finally. This has been almost 200 years in the making. The Gowl-Die has rested for far too long. It is time to bring it back. Where will we be in five years, I'm not sure. But we will have a leader, a protector, a guardian. We can all have more kids once we know we're safe with the Gowl-Die. Now, please dump your vases one at a time on the inner circle, while reciting the slow chant."

First, the participants all started a low, quiet chant. Remembering back to the church incident, I felt my hand burn, and The Mark came to life. There wasn't a headache this time, but the three cuts flowed like infinity pools. To the left of Dr. Montgomery, the first woman stepped forward. While chanting, she pulled the top of the vase and splashed the blood of their own children onto the circle. Immediately, the blood seemed to move and flow to the center, making a disk shape that I was all too familiar with. The next woman went, and the next one, and the next one. The blood of their offspring offered up to some monster that they wanted to please. I couldn't imagine having a kid, let alone killing my own child. I didn't want to think about it, but it was too late.

Lisa stayed strong, but we were both disgusted. Some of the blood would splash back onto our feet and legs, but I was just glad we both had jeans and shoes on. The 18 childless mothers finished throwing the blood in, and the chanting stopped. The blood had originally pooled in the middle of the circle, but now it started to rotate, one line at a time. And each line ended on the sixth portion next to me and Lisa. The portion that assumingly held the symbol of the Gowl-Die.

That section turned dark red with all the blood, and then the blood soaked into the ground instantaneously. Soon after, there was shaking and rumbling while the circle started crumbling. I noticed my feet weren't tied up when Lisa started scooting back from the destruction. I followed suit while Pastor Blackwood and Dr. Montgomery stood in awe, awaiting their god. But as the rumbling ended, there was an eerie quiet that was oddly interrupted.

"Christopher James Walker, are you down there?"

Pastor Blackwood was fuming as he turned to the doorway. Without getting any clarification, a sheriff trotted into the basement with Todd Pickley, Mr. Pickley, Mrs. Pickley, Chief Rykowski, Officer Bailey, and a few other cops I didn't recognize. I wanted to say their presence gave me a sense of relief, but it actually didn't. It meant more people were at risk, and I felt to blame.

As the ground started to rumble once again, Chief Rykowski looked about and saw me tied to a chair.

"What in the blue fuck is going on here?" Chief Rykowski asked.

"Gentlemen, and ladies, you're just in time," Pastor Blackwood said.

"In time for what?" Mr. Pickley asked, and then he saw me. "Oh, you got him tied down for me?"

"Who are you?" Dr. Montgomery asked, without truly caring.

Mr. Pickley showed his vast intelligence by saying, "I'm my son's father. The son that was beaten up by that piece of shit over there!"

Everyone turned to look at me, and I tried waving like a jackass. Todd's nose looked like a deflated elephant trunk, and some big piece of gauze stuck out of his mouth as he tried to speak.

"Fyeah, fat fucking fuy fight fair fknocked fy feeth fout."

"Jesus, Todd, you're sounding as intelligent as always."

"You got some fucking nerve, kid."

Mr. Pickley wanted to storm over to me, but Dr. Montgomery stopped him.

"Do not step near the summoning circle."

"The what?"

"Hey, where's Yamura? Is he here?" Chief Rykowski asked.

"Oh," Thomas' wife started, honing in on her moment of revenge. "He's here, but he's no longer with us."

Rykowski's eyes widened as he reached for his magnum revolver. Dr. Montgomery and the women all pointed their weapons at the Pickleys and the police.

"What the hell are you all doing?" Chief Rykowski clamored.

Even though much more explanation was needed, the ground opened, and rubble flew about, hitting some of the people and making them fall. I took a rock to my bad shoulder and fell back, but that caused my right hand to slip out from its rope. I looked up, while lying on my left side, to see the spectacle of the year.

The Gowl-Die rose from the center, almost like it was being carefully pulled up by a string. Its gray skin was like a hairless cat, and there was a greasy clear liquid running all over its body. Its wings stayed closed and close to its back, and I saw it shake. Placing its feet down, it was hunched over and appeared famished or weak. The police, the Pickleys, Lisa, and I were all scared while the professor and pastor were astonished. The other onlookers had mixed reactions. Some were happy, while others gasped. The rumbling stopped, and the Gowl-Die stayed hunched, looking towards Pastor Blackwood and Dr. Montgomery.

"My, aren't you incredible!" Pastor Blackwood shouted. "I can't believe I'm seeing it with my own two eyes! Our savior has risen."

Todd's mouth was open so wide, his big chunk of gauze fell out. The Gowl-Die appeared timid and slimy. If it was waiting for a greeting, I didn't have one to give it.

"Wow. I can't believe it worked," Dr. Montgomery said. "Now for phase two."

Wanting to ask for clarification, Pastor Blackwood turned to his brother, only to see him raising his pistol. The pastor raised his hand in horror, and Dr. Montgomery fired. The bullet went through the pastor's hand and into the Gowl-Die's head, rendering it deceased.

CHAPTER EIGHTEEN

The Best and Worst Night of My Life

As the Gowl-Die crumpled to the ground, I started to wonder if Dr. Montgomery really was on our side all along. Instead, the reason was much worse.

"Man with The First Mark will take the Gowl-Die's power," Dr. Montgomery said.

I could barely hear him over the pastor's cries in pain. Afraid of what would happen next, I looked at my hand and saw the lines still wavering. I was told I had The Mark, but he never called it The First Mark...

Dropping the pistol, Dr. Montgomery threw his coat to the side, ripped his buttoned shirt, and turned his back to everyone, revealing a larger and uglier version of The Mark all across his back. The four lines on his back were waving and creating a 3D effect. The original Gowl-Die melted in the rubble, and the fluids ran to Dr. Montgomery's back. As they merged into his body, a horrific transformation began. His hair fell out. His jaw cracked and extended while his teeth tripled in length and size. He was laughing as his feet burst through his shoes and became prehistoric-sized talons. His hands shook and morphed from being human hands to large claws. His skin grayed, and the wings began to burst out of his back. It wasn't Dr. Montgomery anymore, it was a stronger, fiercer Gowl-Die.

Pastor Blackwood held his shot hand but stared at his brother in wonderment.

"Brother, why didn't you tell me?" Pastor Blackwood asked. "Now, you can be our leader!"

The Gowl-Die's mouth shook as he made short, rapid breaths. There was a cracking in the back of his throat, and he turned to face

Pastor Blackwood. Everyone was petrified with fear until I saw his eyes flip from black to red.

"Fuck!" I yelled.

Pastor Blackwood turned from a living being to a sack of blood and guts in two swipes. The Gowl-Die's claws were insanely sharp and didn't experience any resistance. Mrs. Pickley screamed as the Gowl-Die dove down into what was Pastor Blackwood and began feasting. As quick as I could, I untied my left arm and ripped the rope off from Lisa's hands.

"Everyone, to the panic room, now!" I shouted.

The screams continued, but the Gowl-Die wasn't finished. It didn't need any followers or help and appeared to be completely fine working alone. All the women who made the ultimate sacrifice froze in place and screamed. It did feel like I couldn't move my legs fast enough, but if Chief Rykowski could haul ass, I could too. Lisa and I entered the panic room first as we saw the Gowl-Die rip and eat one person after another. Each kill gave him more strength, and we couldn't even tell it was Dr. Montgomery anymore. The monster had completely taken him over.

Chief Rykowski, Officer Bailey, the three Pickleys, Lisa, and I all gathered in the panic room. I tried waiting for more to join us, but the other officers began shooting at the beast. Unlike the original Gowl-Die, this one wasn't succumbing to gunfire as easily. It was like they were shooting it with peas, and before we could convince them to join us in the panic room, the sheriff and remaining officers were ripped to shreds.

"Close the goddamn door!" Mr. Pickley shouted.

The Gowl-Die and I locked eyes for a second, and they flipped red again. Before he could fly to the door, I slammed it in his face, and for once, his claws seemed to be unable to pierce through the metal. He tried a few times before giving up and went back to feed on those that perished.

"I see why the church made this room, now," I commented to Lisa.

As I turned away from the door, I found a new enemy fast approaching. Mr. Pickley stepped up, took a swing at my jaw, and I fell to the floor.

"Mr. Pickley, for Christ's sake, that can wait!" Chief Rykowski shouted.

"No, no, this dumb fucking kid, he doesn't know when to quit, does he? Sheriff told us on the way here, he killed two people within a few nights of staying at his aunt and uncle's. We should just throw him out there to that monster."

"No, you wouldn't want to do that," Lisa said. "That will grant the Gowl-Die its full strength."

"What now?"

"That thing, out there? That used to be my grandpa? It's called a Gowl-Die. It's an ancient monster that was sealed away hundreds of years ago, but this godforsaken town resurrected it. I didn't know my grandpa also had The Mark, and based on what he said, he got it before yours. That means the power of the Gowl-Die was split between three entities. If we feed Chris to the Gowl-Die, it'll be able to cut into this room without an issue," Lisa explained.

"Now the truth is told," I said, rubbing my jaw. "But if we kill the Gowl-Die, the power will then transfer to me? Either way, I'm a liability."

"Glad you can recognize that," Mr. Pickley said.

"Boys!" Lisa shouted, and everyone fell silent. Well, except for Todd and his mother, who were rocking back and forth in tears. "We can't fight amongst one another. We need to stay quiet, wait for the Gowl-Die to leave, and then we'll make our way to the surface."

"And then we book it out of here?" Mr. Pickley suggested.

"No," Lisa said, "we're going to kill it, and make sure it doesn't transfer to Chris."

Even with a sore jaw, I managed to smile when she and I locked eyes.

"Aw, that's cute and all. But how the fuck?"

"We're all going to die!" Mrs. Pickley screamed.

The Gowl-Die heard her and tried swiping at the door again, but we seemed to still be safe. The screech it gave off rang a bell, and I realized it was the same shriek from the night one of the chickens got ripped up through the fence. Could the Gowl-Die scream through several layers of the ground?

"Did you not hear me? I said be quiet," Lisa seethed through gritted teeth.

Todd and Mrs. Pickley had completely lost it, while Mr. Pickley's top priority was still to beat the snot out of me. Finally, instead of staring me down, he went over to his wife and son and tried to comfort them, like a lion to mice. Outside of the panic room, we heard the Gowl-Die feasting upon the separate bodies, taking its time. With the sound of each bone snapping in its jaws, we all shuddered and waited for a clear path.

"Yamura," Chief Rykowski said softly. "Did the pastor kill him?"

"No, Dr. Montgomery did," I replied.

It seemed that when we talked low, the Gowl-Die didn't care to try and break in again. I had to guess that Dr. Montgomery's consciousness was completely out the window, and that the Gowl-Die took over any and all feelings and desires he once had.

"Turns out, my grandpa and Pastor Blackwood are half-brothers," Lisa explained, still in denial. "They must have been planning this for years. I think I was meant to be the original sacrifice, but..."

"Sweetheart," Officer Bailey said.

"So, what the hell is a Gowl-Die?" Mr. Pickley asked, finally lowering the volume of his voice.

"A gowl is a loud cry, while die is, well, you know. But they named it that because, in its original form, it was able to produce a scream that would disorient or scramble the brain of its victim before ripping them apart."

"But he can't make that scream because of Chris?" Mr. Pickley followed up.

"Exactly. If Chris were to die, too, the Gowl-Die would have its full strength and power. It'd be able to produce the gowl, while also being able to cut through this room and most other objects in the world."

"So, I'll ask again. How do we kill it?"

"As soon as we think the coast is clear, we can run up to my uncle's bedroom. He has plenty of guns and ammo we can distribute. Hell, he has some guns down in the basement as well," I offered.

"Didn't look like the cops could shoot it," Mr. Pickley scowled.

"Nine-millimeter probably isn't doing the trick," Chief Rykowski replied. "I have my 357 revolver here, and a pump shotgun out in my car. When the coast is clear, we'll run out to my car. Oh, and we can check the sheriff's car and the other car that came up here."

"If I had brought my truck, I'd have a few weapons to choose from," Mr. Pickley sighed. Then, looking at me, he asked, "Do you have a gun you can spare me?"

"Yeah, as long as you don't shoot me in the back of the head," I commented.

"If you can get us out of here alive, I'll spare you the beating and re-hire your father."

"Deal."

Mr. Pickley reached out his hand, and we shook on it. At about that same time, we heard someone shout from above ground, and it alerted the Gowl-Die. The men were still alive, but they probably wouldn't live very long.

With Lisa leading the pack, she approached the door and cautiously pushed it open. Once she noticed the coast was clear, she called out, "Alright, cops go to the cars, the rest of us will go to his uncle's bedroom. Once we're all armed, let's try to spread out and hit it from different angles. Anyone who doesn't think they can fight should stay down here. Chris, I'll need you near me, in case the fusion starts after we kill it. Everyone understand? Let's move."

Mr. Pickley looked to his son, but he wouldn't budge. I saw a sense of disappointment on his face since he hoped to fight the monster with his son. Instead, Mr. Pickley turned to me and Lisa and said, "They can stay down here. I'll follow you two."

Leaving Todd and Mrs. Pickley in the panic room made the most sense as the rest of us piled out of the panic room. I glanced at the gun safe in the basement and noticed it was already raided. Maybe Uncle Bob had been storing all the guns for the neighborhood. I just hoped his bedroom was untouched. Stepping over the mushy bodies, I saw a pistol and grabbed it. It was the 1911 pistol that was missing from my satchel. It appeared Lisa was telling the truth about not knowing where it went. That gave me at least some closure.

When we reached the surface, we saw a massive Gowl-Die shaped hole in the garage door like some kind of cartoon. Not paying it too much mind, we heard gunfire and screams from the streets of the neighborhood. They sounded distant, so we all felt safe for now as we ran out. Following the plan, Chief Rykowski and Officer Bailey made their way to the patrol cars while Lisa, Mr. Pickley, and I headed towards my uncle's bedroom. The gun safe's door was barely ajar, but a wash of relief came over me as we opened the door and found most of the guns still present. Including my uncle's 10-gauge shotgun.

I grabbed it and found a belt with a holster and more ammo for the 1911. With a quick clip and adjustment, I was battle-ready. Lisa grabbed a lever-action rifle with a handful of bullets, while Mr. Pickley grabbed the M16A2.

"Man, haven't held one of these since I was in the service," he commented.

"Vietnam?"

"Yeah, as a mechanic in the Navy."

"Cool."

"Yeah, let's chat later," Lisa urged as she grabbed a few grenades and threw them in a nearby backpack.

I grabbed a few as well, some looked like fragmentation while the rest were smoke. Still wondering how my uncle got all of this, I shook my head and felt as ready as I could be. Armed to the teeth, we went out the front door to join the others.

In shock and awe, we saw the Gowl-Die taking flight to avoid the myriad of bullets trying to take it down. The summoners were now the aggressors. A few small fires had broken out, possibly where the torch holders dropped them. Some of the neighbors rode around in a modified truck with a mounted gun, trying to take down the Gowl-Die. When that gun seemed to be doing the trick, the Gowl-Die made quick work of it, diving down and slicing through the center of the truck. Blood and limbs ejected about, and the Gowl-Die went airborne once more.

Chief Rykowski and Officer Bailey ignored the spectacle as they ran up to us.

"Okay, we have some firepower," the chief said, then he noticed out loadouts. "What the hell. I'm going to have a talk with your uncle when this is over."

Lisa reached into her backpack and distributed a few grenades to the two police officers. In any other context, none of this would make sense. But we had a monster to deal with.

"If the Gowl Die is zeroing in on you, use the smoke grenade. Otherwise, only use a frag when he's out a ways from other people." Lisa then mimed the motions of handling a grenade. "Keep hold of the handle when pulling the pin. Once the handle is released, you have five seconds to take cover."

"Can these blow up cars?" I asked.

"No, that's only in the movies," Mr. Pickley answered. "But if we're thinking of using fire to kill this thing, we should try and prime some cars to explode. Maybe lure it towards one."

"There's gas in my uncle's garage," I pointed.

The Gowl-Die dove once more, taking out two men in one swipe. There were only a few churchgoers left alive, and they couldn't take their eyes off of it.

"Right, just don't rig the vehicles we came in on. We'll start checking garages to see who has gasoline," Chief Rykowski offered. "And as crazy as these people are, return fire only. I don't want anyone gunning them down unless they start it, got it?"

"Right," Lisa replied.

"Move out!"

Deciding we had chattered enough, it was time to act. Lisa and I bolted to my uncle's garage while Rykowski and Bailey ran to the houses across the street. Mr. Pickley stood guard by my uncle's house. The Gowl-Die had torn into a few houses, easily cutting through brick. But as I observed more and more, it appeared that metal was the only substance the Gowl-Die had a hard time with. I slung the shotgun behind my back and offered to run with the gasoline cans while Lisa provided me cover. The Gowl-Die was flying towards the other end of the neighborhood, not interested in our antics. Some of the disciples stopped shooting aimlessly at it and decided to take cover in the houses to regroup. Their distraction was nice while it lasted, but we were out of luck.

"Let's soak that car over there."

Lisa had pointed to the car next to my uncle's house. I nodded, and we made our way to the sedan. It was the house where the kid kept calling me the new one. I knew what he meant now, but I would never see him again.

There was a thud far away from us, and I saw the Gowl-Die perch on the house next to the pastor's. No one was shooting at him, so now it had to look for the next victim.

"Can it see this far away?" I asked.

"It is nocturnal in nature. Go ahead and throw a smoke grenade."

I tossed one into the street, and it slowly fumigated. I could only hope it was enough to cover us as I grabbed a gas can and opened the top. With shaking hands, I started dumping the gas over the car. I didn't realize how much I dumped until Lisa scolded, "Hey, don't waste it all on one car. We need to ration in."

"Right."

I stopped and we headed towards the next house closer to the neighborhood entrance. Looking back, I saw Rykowski and Bailey attempting to soak a car, but they were having the same issue as me. Bailey scolded him, too, so I guess I'm just glad we had the women with us.

Pouring gasoline on the next car, I found that we were already down a can. Cursing at myself, I threw the can aside and told Lisa we should move on. The Gowl-Die sat, still perched on the house, still looking about. It didn't seem like something that could get tired, but I figured if it wasn't at full strength, maybe it could be.

When we ran up to the second to last house, I started pouring the gas into the flatbed of a parked truck. Lisa was keeping an eye out, but we didn't think to look back at the house.

"What're you doing to my truck?"

Coming off as famous last words, I turned to the house and watched as a man with a rifle stared out from his front door. Recalling what Chief Rykowski ordered, I dropped the can but didn't draw the shotgun.

"I forgot the owners might still be alive," I muttered to Lisa.

The man wouldn't break eye contact, and I saw his jaw drop as he continued looking at me.

"The one who bears The Mark must die!"

"Shit."

The man was able to fire off a few shots. First hitting the concrete in front of us, then the car. Enough sparks flew up that the truck swiftly ignited. I left the gas can behind as Lisa fired off two rounds from the lever action. The first hit near the man's head, while the next one hit his arm as he turned away. Lisa was able to add a few more bullets into the side loader before ejecting the last round fired. Deciding to get far away from the truck, we crossed the street to intercept the chief.

"Did you soak some cars over here?" Lisa asked.

"Yeah, but I don't think we discussed how to light them," Chief Rykowski said.

In poor timing, an explosion occurred behind us as the truck erupted. Lisa was the only one who didn't flinch. A few windows shattered at the nearby houses, and I made a face.

"Well, shoot them until there are sparks," I suggested.

"Hey, here it comes!" Mr. Pickley shouted from my uncle's.

The Gowl-Die stood tall and shook its wings before taking flight. Mr. Pickley fired towards it, and it headed straight for him.

"Run!" I yelled.

Stopping his fire, he ran towards the front door, and the Gowl-Die dragged its claws all along the front of the house. Weirdly enough, it didn't seem as zeroed in anymore on killing us measly people. Instead, once it was done remodeling my uncle's house, it turned towards me, and the eyes turned red. Holding the shotgun, I turned to the house we were at and blasted the front door open. Feeling the wind from its wings, we ran into the house. Not a single light was on, but there wasn't time to start flicking every switch. Lisa and I ran down the hallway, then turned to go upstairs. Chief Rykowski and Officer Bailey split left into a different hallway, and the Gowl-Die broke through the front entryway with ease. I saw it standing at the doorway, and his eyes stayed red as they scanned the house. I was pushing my luck by seeing them turn red so many times without dying that I told myself to focus and followed Lisa. The Gowl-Die leapt forward into the hallway and attacked underneath the stairs. Feeling the floor weaken beneath me got me moving. I made it to the top and fired the shotgun at it. Damaging the left wing, the Gowl-Die cried out and stuck to the ground for now.

"Nice shot," Lisa commented.

We stood at the top of the stairs, watching it. Even if it couldn't fly, we quickly learned it could climb. Smacking its claws into the wall, it slowly but surely made its way up to us, and we ran down the upstairs hallway. I screamed as I ran, knowing that it wanted me. Reaching the end of the hallway, we burst into the last room on the right and prayed it had a window. The Gowl-Die was a slow runner, but its thudding against the floor was pulsating and unsettling. I closed the door, even though it wouldn't help much, and we checked around the kid's bedroom. Lisa turned to me and yelled, "Hey, blow out this window. We'll have to jump."

The Gowl-Die slashed the door while I shot out the window. It didn't break cleanly, and I knew we'd get scratched up. Turning to face the Gowl-Die, I pumped and fired the shotgun four more times. The shells were tearing him up, and saliva started expelling from his mouth. Its head was shaking, with the jaw bouncing up and down.

Lisa sat on the window sill before jumping out. I looked out to see her tuck and roll gracefully. I knew I wasn't going to land like that. Once she was out of the way, I jumped and felt a burning sensation across my back as I fell. The Gowl-Die took a swipe at me but came up a little short. When I landed, my right ankle rolled, and I crumbled to the ground.

"Chris, get the fuck up, now!"

As always, Lisa had a way to call my attention. I ignored the burning on my back as blood ran down, along with the pain in my ankle. Now in the backyard, we ran around a tree to try and get back to the front. The Gowl-Die lifted the claw that cut me and let the blood drip into its mouth, but ended up screaming and shivering.

"What the hell," I commented.

Lisa kicked the nice wooden gate open and said, "You've hurt it really good, so it needs to feed again. But, it can't feed off of your blood since you have The Mark. It's like cannibalism to him."

"Glad the Gowl-Die has some morals."

"The jokes just don't quit with you, do they?"

"Keeps my mind off of dying."

Her silence didn't surprise me as we rounded the front of the house. Expecting to see Chief Rykowski and Officer Bailey, we only saw Mr. Pickley across the street.

"It's wounded upstairs!" Lisa shouted across the street.

Soon after, Chief Rykowski and Officer Bailey rushed out and tried to approach us. But before they could, the Gowl-Die dropped like a hawk on top of Chief Rykowski. He fell forward while Officer Bailey kept running, and then the Gowl-Die leaned over him to slowly cut open the back of his head from ear to ear. Rykowski's scream would have to act as his final words as blood poured out for the Gowl-Die. Officer Bailey turned and couldn't act. Lisa raised her rifle and fired at the Gowl-Die as it tried to feast. It ate just enough blood and brain to regenerate its bum wing, but the center of the beast was still torn from my shotgun. It took flight, and even though I was ready to run, Officer Bailey went to pay respects to her chief.

"We have to move," Lisa urged.

"No, I have a better idea," I said.

The Gowl-Die circled by the pastor's house once again, and I dropped the shotgun to run to one of the rigged cars. Lisa, Officer Bailey, and Mr. Pickley watched me in confusion. Truth was, I didn't want to see any more people die. Even if it was one of the idiots that caused this mess. I was ready to kill the Gowl-Die, and in turn, kill myself.

"Hey, come back here!" I yelled at the Gowl-Die. "It's me you want, right? I have The Mark. Come and get it!"

"Chris, no!" Lisa shouted.

"I have a plan, trust me."

"Yeah, to get yourself killed!"

Mr. Pickley realized what I was doing as well, and said, "Chris, son, don't do it. I want to bring you back to your parents in one piece."

That bastard was sincere, and I hated it. But it wasn't the time to get mushy gushy. I felt The Mark and was accepting my fate.

"If I'm going to turn into the Gowl-Die anyway, might as well blow both of us up at the same time."

Loving that I was alone, The Gowl-Die swooped down towards me. The Gowl-Die, formerly known as Dr. Montgomery, was eager to slice me to bits and gain full power.

I stood next to the rigged car, without a care in the world. It felt good to go out like a hero. But in a last-second revision to my plan, I pulled the 1911 pistol out and fired up at the Gowl-Die. I wasn't the only one. Mr. Pickley, Officer Bailey, and Lisa all fired as well, and where the Gowl-Die was once planning to swipe, it veered to the side and smashed into the rigged car. The force from its fall knocked me down, and I turned to watch. Raising my pistol, I was ready to fire and cause the spark, but I was out of bullets.

"No, no, no, no," I fussed.

As steam and dust rose from the car, Lisa ran up to me and started pulling me away from the car. Mr. Pickley helped her as Officer Bailey threw a few grenades on top of the car.

"No, what are you doing? I have to die with it!" I shouted.

"You'll see," Lisa replied confidently.

As soon as we were seemingly far enough from it, the Gowl-Die slowly tried to lift itself from the car. Our bullets had almost defeated it, but there was still one last thing to do.

Blow it up.

Mr. Pickley took out a small matchbook and struck one on the first attempt. The Gowl-Die didn't seem any the wiser as its eyes stayed black. It looked like a hurt animal, but we weren't going to fall for it. Mr. Pickley tossed the match, and the Gowl-Die went up in flames. It started screeching and shrieking, and only stopped when the grenades started to go off, slicing it up into pieces. Just like that, it was gone.

But there's an odd feeling about accepting death and then not dying. I felt a bit empty, as I was fully committed to being in the flames with the Gowl-Die. I thought about jumping in, but for some reason, everyone was waiting.

"No, it's happening!" Officer Bailey cried.

From the flames, an indistinguishable liquid flowed towards me. Neither hot nor cold, it rushed onto my body and started pouring into The Mark. The Mark seemed to widen and wanted to distort, and I felt my blood thicken. I couldn't breathe, and I saw Officer Bailey and Mr. Pickley point their guns at me.

"Wait, don't shoot him!" Lisa pleaded.

"But, you said it yourself. He will become the Gowl-Die!" Officer Bailey argued.

"Kill me!" I yelled. "I feel my body changing. Please, kill me!"

"Lisa, this is insane. We have to kill him before he changes. Otherwise, he'll be more powerful than your grandpa."

"No," she said, and she pointed down to me. "Look."

As the liquid thickly flowed under my skin, I felt it inhabit my legs, my torso, and my arms. My spine started to curve, and the back of my head was pulsing. But something did seem off. Dr. Montgomery distorted so quickly compared to me. I didn't see why Lisa wouldn't let them shoot me until a bright beam of light shone from my left hand. With all my might, I lowered my head and saw the ring she had given me was glowing with the strength of the sun. Not worried about losing our eyesights, we stared at the orange beam of light, and my body started to feel no pain. Without any effort on my part, the liquid seemed to shift gears and rush to my pinky finger. My blood flow started to feel normal again, and it appeared the ring was sucking all the bad fluids out of me. The ring didn't expand or seem to waver, but I felt a sense of relief as the thick liquids left my body. I was just Chris once again.

When the ring finished, it stopped shining and returned to normal. Lisa walked up to me, pulled the ring off, and threw it in the fire. My right hand was healed. I no longer had The Mark.

"Uh, what?" Mr. Pickley asked.

"My mother gave me that ring. She said an absorbing spell was used on it centuries ago, supposedly repelling evil magic."

"And you knew that would stop the Gowl-Die from transferring to me?" I asked.

"Well, I didn't actually know if it would work."

"What!" Officer Bailey yelled.

"Hey, sometimes you gotta try things and just hope for the best," Lisa said with a shrug.

Part of me was furious, but the alive and well part of me stood up and wrapped my arms around her tightly. Now I knew I could really trust her.

Now What?

A few weeks later...

No amount of time could ever make things feel normal. After the incident, Mr. Pickley offered to drive me back home to Lawton, but I wanted to stay with Lisa. Mr. Pickley understood, and we shook hands before he left. He promised up and down my dad would get his job back, and I believed him. I also took the house-sitting money and sent it back with him, asking if he could give it to my mom.

Todd had nothing else to say to me, which worked out since his front teeth were missing, and I could barely understand what he was saying at any given time. Either way, the hatchet was buried. No more worrying about my dad not having a job, or my teeth not having a mouth.

Officer Bailey was distraught, to say the least. Losing two friends in one night couldn't have been easy, and I didn't know what she would do going forward. She wanted to report the incident to the FBI, but what the hell would they even think? She figured they'd throw us all in the loony bin, so she stayed quiet.

My aunt and uncle did return home, only to grab Mr. Pickles and look for a new place to live. Their house wasn't completely ruined, but it'd still be a nightmare to sell. I can only assume having a monster summoned in your basement hurts the resale value.

Then, there was Lisa, who still felt the betrayal of her grandpa like a fresh wound. It still didn't make sense to her, but I tried to make her feel better while I stayed at her house. One suggestion was to take down all photos of her grandpa, which she was more than willing to do. But she wasn't ready to destroy any of them. He did protect and train her for ten years, after all. Only to be engulfed with the idea of summoning an ancient monster, just so he could take its power. Yeah, maybe everlasting life was cool, but not as a freak.

Lisa took over her grandpa's bedroom, and I stayed in the second guest room. We stayed up late, talking and sharing stories. Sometimes we fell asleep, holding each other on the couch. Sometimes we ended up in one or the other bedroom. It all felt right, but neither of us had used the L word yet.

She suggested books for me to read on how to become a Tracker. Some days, she trained me in the backyard to further my combat skills. Other days, she wanted to be alone. I inherited her grandfather's car and was able to drive into town sometimes. Not that there was much to see, but it gave me something to do when Lisa needed her time.

We attended the funeral of Chief Rykowski and Detective Yamura. The town was confused by their causes of death, and that was when we told them the lie of how they died. I couldn't imagine how they'd react to the truth.

But after the funeral, Officer Bailey followed us to Ruby Falls to sit and talk with us. After a cup of coffee, she spilled her feelings.

"I think when I'm done training this new group, I'm going to quit."

"Quit?" I asked. "Not even just transfer to a different department?"

"No, I can't even fathom trying to be a plainclothes officer anymore. Even if I could find a town smaller than this, there might be even more fucked-up shit there. I came out here thinking it wouldn't be as bad as the big city. But after this..."

"I get it, don't feel the need to explain yourself," Lisa said.

"Oh yeah, make me look like the bad guy," I complained.

"You almost were."

"Ouch."

We sat in the cozy living room, happy to have some company. Even under the circumstances.

"Well, what about you two? You're practically still kids. You just going to live out here on your grandpa's property?"

"Property? You just mean this house, right?"

"Well, no," Officer Bailey said, and she adjusted herself. "Your grandpa never actually sold the land. Hank Blackwood just started building all the houses with the professor's permission. So, since you're inheriting this house, you actually own Ruby Falls."

"Hey, that's awesome!" I said. "So, we can go around and start demolishing the other houses? Oh, I say we destroy the church first."

"You may want to ask Lisa. Oh, and your uncle. Has he moved everything out yet?"

"No," I replied.

"I agree, church first. Maybe your uncle's house after," Lisa sneered.

"But seriously, what are you two going to do?" Officer Bailey asked.

Not seeing a reason to lie, Lisa said, "I'm training him to be a Tracker. Just like me."

"A Tracker?"

Lisa explained the best she could about how Trackers are supposed to find the unknown evils of the great plains. Intrigued, Officer Bailey replied, "Well, that actually sounds... really interesting. I suppose you don't offer a pension plan, though, right?"

"Not yet," Lisa joked.

"Well, as soon as I train these new recruits, and we get a new chief in place, I'm in. But maybe I can test out of the basics with my current experience."

"Oh yeah, I know you'll do a lot better than him."

We shared a laugh, but it was interrupted by a loud engine outside. We all sat up at alert and shared a look of confusion.

"Is that a helicopter?" Officer Bailey asked.

Deciding to check it out, the ladies made their way outside, but my stomach suddenly turned. Running to the nearest bathroom, I dropped my head into the sink and started gagging. Eventually, I coughed up a black sludge that slowly crept down the drain. I saw stars and took a few breaths before exiting. And as much as I hate to say it, this wasn't the first time something like that had happened since the incident.

Trying to ignore it, I stepped outside to see an unmarked helicopter grounded in front of the house. A few men stepped out, and one held a nice metal suitcase. I felt I was interrupting a conversation as I stepped out.

Lisa turned back to me with a smile and said, "Chris, these men are Trackers, too. They asked us to join them."

Figuring I was ready for a new adventure, I nodded and said, "When do we start?"

The End...?

Henry Cline is an Oklahoma-based author, musician, and songwriter. Henry was born in November of 1994, in Oklahoma City, Oklahoma. Henry began scribbling his thoughts at age seven, but by age 11, he wrote his first novel. 12 years later in February of 2017, he was picked up by Sands Press. Current releases include the gangster epic The Platinum Briefcase and the multiple entries in the Jack Sampson Mysteries Series.

As a musician, he's released two studio albums, Resilience and Connections. Follow @thehenrycline on all socials for future news and releases.

LinkedIn:
https://www.linkedin.com/in/henry-cline-045b0b61/
Facebook:
www.facebook.com/thehenrycline
Instagram:
www.instagram.com/Thehenrycline

www.ingramcontent.com/pod-product-compliance
Lightning Source LLC
Chambersburg PA
CBHW060452310726
48977CB00001B/409